THE C[...]
SPRINGFIELD [P9-DOC-110]

Marci fingered the sample packet of antibiotic, her manner once more wary. "I'm not in the habit of accepting favors."

"No strings attached, okay?" Christopher held her gaze for a long moment, willing her to believe that not all men were untrustworthy.

Marci searched his eyes, and after a few seconds he detected an almost imperceptible softening in her features.

He headed toward the door, and she stood to trail behind him. Pausing on the threshold, he withdrew a card from his pocket and handed it to her. "If you feel worse or things don't improve by tomorrow, call me."

A few seconds ticked by as she read the card. Blinked. Swallowed. Lifting her chin, she looked into his eyes. "Thank you, Doctor."

The words, delivered in a soft, shy tone, revealed an unexpected and touching... vulnerability.

Discarded by the City Library

THE CITY LIBRARY
SPRINGFIELD (MA) CITY LIBRARY

Books by Irene Hannon

Steeple Hill Love Inspired

*Home for the Holidays
*A Groom of Her Own
*A Family to Call Her Own
It Had to Be You
One Special Christmas
The Way Home
Never Say Goodbye
Crossroads
**The Best Gift
**Gift from the Heart
**The Unexpected Gift

All Our Tomorrows
The Family Man
Rainbow's End
†From This Day Forward
†A Dream To Share
†Where Love Abides
Apprentice Father
††Tides of Hope
††The Hero Next Door
††The Doctor's Perfect Match

*Vows
**Sisters & Brides
†Heartland Homecomings
††Lighthouse Lane

IRENE HANNON

Irene Hannon, who writes both romance and romantic suspense, is the bestselling author of more than thirty novels. Her books have been honored with the coveted RITA® Award from Romance Writers of America (the "Oscar" of romantic fiction), the HOLT Medallion and the Reviewer's Choice Award from *RT Book Reviews*.

A former corporate communications executive with a Fortune 500 company, Irene now writes full-time. In her spare time, she enjoys singing, traveling, long walks, cooking, gardening and spending time with family. She and her husband make their home in Missouri.

For more information about her and her books, Irene invites you to visit her Web site at www.irenehannon.com.

The Doctor's Perfect Match

Irene Hannon

Steeple
Hill®

Published by Steeple Hill Books™

If you purchased this book without a cover you should be aware
that this book is stolen property. It was reported as "unsold and
destroyed" to the publisher, and neither the author nor the
publisher has received any payment for this "stripped book."

STEEPLE HILL BOOKS

**Steeple
Hill®**

Recycling programs
for this product may
not exist in your area.

ISBN-13: 978-0-373-81450-3

THE DOCTOR'S PERFECT MATCH

Copyright © 2010 by Irene Hannon

All rights reserved. Except for use in any review, the reproduction
or utilization of this work in whole or in part in any form by any
electronic, mechanical or other means, now known or hereafter
invented, including xerography, photocopying and recording, or in
any information storage or retrieval system, is forbidden without
the written permission of the editorial office, Steeple Hill Books,
233 Broadway, New York, NY 10279 U.S.A.

This is a work of fiction. Names, characters, places and incidents are
either the product of the author's imagination or are used fictitiously, and
any resemblance to actual persons, living or dead, business establishments,
events or locales is entirely coincidental.

This edition published by arrangement with Steeple Hill Books.

® and TM are trademarks of Steeple Hill Books, used under license.
Trademarks indicated with ® are registered in the United States Patent
and Trademark Office, the Canadian Trade Marks Office and in other
countries.

www.SteepleHill.com

Printed in U.S.A.

I pray that the eyes of your heart may be
enlightened, so that you will
know what is the hope of his calling.
—*Ephesians* 1:18

To Jo Ann Case—
My forever-young friend.
Happy 90th birthday!

Prologue

The woman was crying.

Christopher Morgan gave the blonde at the dim corner table a discreet glance over the rim of his coffee cup. He'd noticed her earlier, when the hostess had shown him to his favorite tucked-away table in the Nantucket eatery. With her pinup figure, slightly frizzy chin-length flaxen hair and emerald-colored eyes, she was hard to miss.

Yet the other patrons at the popular restaurant seemed oblivious to her. And to her distress. They were all focused on their companions.

He, on the other hand, was alone.

As was the woman.

His gaze swung back to her as she turned away from her bowl of half-eaten chowder to rummage in her purse, the sheen on her cheeks mute testimony to her misery.

Frowning, Christopher set his cup back on the saucer. He'd always been a sucker for people in need. That was one of the reasons he'd become a doctor. But despite his humanitarian inclinations, it wasn't wise to offer assistance to strangers these days. Magnanimous gestures like that could arouse resentment or suspicion, or worse.

An image of his former girlfriend, Denise, flashed through his mind, and his gut twisted into a painful knot. He'd followed his compassionate instincts with her, and that traumatic experience had taught him a valuable lesson: crying women were a disaster waiting to happen. The safest course was to steer a wide berth around them.

Besides, after a busy shift in the E.R., he was in no mood to tiptoe through the minefield the blonde in the corner booth no doubt represented.

He watched as she dabbed away the evidence of her tears with a tissue, tucked it back in her purse and withdrew a ten-dollar bill. Laying it on the table, she scooted to the edge of the booth and swiveled on the seat.

Christopher started to glance away, but as the clingy fabric of her black cocktail dress inched up he found himself mesmerized by the best pair of legs he'd ever seen.

He wasn't certain how long he stared at her, but suddenly the woman rose and yanked her skirt down until the hem brushed the top of her knees.

Looking up at her face, Christopher found her glaring at him, the color high in her cheeks as she tugged at a modest neckline below a single strand of pearls. Heat crept up his neck, fueled by embarrassment and regret. Not only did he feel like a teenage boy, he'd also made her uncomfortable.

And something more, he realized as their gazes locked for a brief moment.

She looked hurt. Defeated. And once again on the verge of tears.

Turning her back on him, she took the long way around the room to the door to avoid passing his table.

After swigging the rest of his coffee, Christopher settled his bill and headed toward the exit, wishing he could replay the last few minutes. He was supposed to be in the business of alleviating suffering, not creating it. But tonight he'd failed miserably.

Stepping out the door, he discovered that dark clouds had replaced the bright, sunny skies on this late May evening. A steady rain had also begun to fall, compelling the strollers and sightseers to seek refuge in the shops and restaurants that lined the streets in the heart of the old town.

All except one.

As Christopher drove up Main Street, he spotted a lone figure trudging through the rain. A blonde in a black cocktail dress.

The woman from the restaurant.

She didn't have an umbrella. Yet she wasn't hurrying. It was as if she were completely unaware of the weather.

Slowing the car, Christopher watched in alarm as she stumbled in her high heels on the uneven brick sidewalk. Walking around Nantucket in shoes like that was an accident waiting to happen, as he well knew. He'd treated any number of women who'd chosen fashion over comfort.

But she righted herself and moved on.

As he approached his turnoff to Orange Street, she continued on Main, her shoulders slumped. She paid no attention to the low rumble of thunder that reverberated through the still air, or the flash of lightning that zigzagged across the sky in the distance. She was either oblivious to the storm—or she didn't care about the danger, Christopher concluded.

Both scenarios disturbed him.

Torn, he watched as she veered left on Fair Street and disappeared from view, the story of the Good Samaritan echoing in his mind. Like the traveler to Jericho who had been beset by thieves, this woman seemed in need of a helping hand.

But so had Denise.

Shoring up his resolve, Christopher turned left onto Orange Street and headed toward 'Sconset, determined to put as much distance as possible between himself and the troubled blonde.

Yet as the miles slipped by, he discovered it wasn't quite as easy to distance himself from the image of those defeated green eyes.

Chapter One

"Are you getting a cold, dear?"

Stifling a sneeze, Marci Clay continued to wash the china plates by hand as Edith Shaw, her new sister-in-law's Lighthouse Lane neighbor, bustled in from The Devon Rose's dining room with another tray of glasses. It had taken them all afternoon and into the early evening to put the tearoom back in order after yesterday afternoon's wedding reception.

"I hope not."

"You've been working too hard since you've been here." Edith tut-tutted as she slid the tray onto the stainless-steel food-prep station in the middle of the kitchen. "It was a very generous gesture, offering to manage the tearoom while Heather and J.C. are on their honeymoon. But that's a lot to take on with very little preparation."

In hindsight, Marci had to admit Edith was right. Given her meager cash reserves, however, it had been the best wedding gift she'd been able to offer. Volunteering to keep Heather's tearoom running during their absence had allowed her brother and his bride to take a longer honeymoon—a gift they'd assured her was priceless. And with her just-earned diploma in hand and no job yet lined up, she had the time.

She'd also assumed her years of waitressing experience would be a sufficient background for the duties at The Devon Rose. But during her indoctrination last week under Heather's tutelage, she'd quickly realized that the world of high tea and Ronnie's Diner were at opposite ends of the spectrum.

The only thing that had kept her from panicking was Edith's willingness to help—plus the invaluable support of Heather's capable assistant, Julie Watson. Knowing she could count on those two women to back her up, Marci had convinced herself she could pull this off.

What she hadn't counted on was getting a cold.

"Having a few second thoughts?"

At Edith's question, Marci regarded the older woman. Her short contemporary hairstyle might feature silvery gray locks, but she radiated youthful energy, and her eyes sparkled with enthusiasm—and insight.

"Maybe." Marci shoved a springy curl out of her eye with the back of her wet hand. "I've done a lot of waitressing, and I'm a decent cook, but this is a really high-class operation. I feel a little out of my league among all this linen and fine china and sterling silver."

"Join the club." Edith chuckled and planted her hands on her ample hips. "I'm more of a chilidog-and-French-fry gal myself. And I'm sure Emily Post or Miss Manners would have a field day critiquing my table etiquette. But if I can get the hang of this tea thing, you can, too."

"I appreciate the encouragement." The words came out scratchy as Marci continued to work her way through the pile of plates.

"Goodness!" Edith gave a sympathetic shake of her head. "I hate to say it, but that sounds like the beginning of a cold to me."

"I think I'm just tired." She'd been working extra hours at Ronnie's to build up her anemic savings account, had stayed up late and consumed far too much caffeine studying for finals and finishing term papers, then had rushed off to Nantucket to learn the ropes at The Devon Rose and participate in all the wedding festivities.

The walk home in the rain last night from the restaurant hadn't helped, either. She should never have indulged in that pity party—nor let regrets about her own bad choices overshadow her joy in J.C.'s well-deserved happiness.

"I'll tell you what." Edith surveyed the kitchen. "We've got most of the mess cleaned up. The tearoom's closed tomorrow and Tuesday, so there's nothing urgent that needs to be done today. Why don't you turn in and let me finish up? It's better to throw off a cold early than to run yourself down and end up sicker."

That was true, Marci conceded. Besides, she was feeling more lethargic by the minute.

"If you're sure you don't mind, I think I will."

"Of course I don't mind." Edith shooed her away from the dishwasher and pushed up the sleeves of her I ♥ Nantucket sweatshirt. "Heather's been like a daughter to me, and with her married to J.C. now, that makes you family. And families help each other out."

Not all families, Marci amended in silence as she thanked Edith and headed upstairs. Hers hadn't been anything like that. Except for J.C., who'd stuck by his brother and sister even through the dark times, despite their efforts to push him away.

Now, thanks to him, she and Nathan had gotten their acts together. But they both had a lot to make up for on the one-for-all, all-for-one front. That's why she was determined to follow through on her commitment to keep The Devon Rose running during J.C. and Heather's absence.

Crawling into bed, Marci pulled the covers up to her chin, closed her eyes and hoped that whatever bug was trying to establish a toehold would give up and retreat.

* * *

"Thanks for stopping by, Christopher. Sorry to interrupt your holiday weekend."

Christopher frowned as he followed Edith to the front door of her house. What holiday?

Then it dawned on him. This was Memorial Day, a time of fun—and rest—for most people. For him, it was just another workday.

"No problem, Edith. I needed to come into town anyway to visit a few patients in the hospital. And I'm on duty in the E.R. later."

"Don't you ever take a day off?"

He smiled. "Now and then."

Shaking her head, she stopped at the door, her hand on the knob. "You know what they say about all work and no play."

"I'll keep that in mind."

"You do that. Anyway, I hated to call you, but Kate worries so much about Maddie that I get paranoid over even the slightest sniffle when I'm babysitting the girls."

After his numerous visits to Kate's small cottage, which was tucked between Edith's house and The Devon Rose, Christopher was well aware of the charter-fishing captain's worries about her daughter. "It's better to err on the side of caution with asthma. I'm glad it was a false alarm." Shifting his black medical bag from one hand to the other, he checked his watch. "I'd better be off if I want to get to the E.R. on time."

To his surprise, Edith didn't budge. "I hate to delay you any further, but I'm a little concerned about Heather's new sister-in-law."

"Heather Anderson? From The Devon Rose?" He saw the tearoom owner regularly at church, though they weren't well acquainted.

"Yes."

"She got married this weekend, didn't she?"

"Yes. A small, intimate wedding. Very romantic."

"What's the problem with her sister-in-law?"

"I hope nothing. She's supposed to manage the tearoom while Heather and J.C. are in Europe on their honeymoon, but yesterday she seemed to be getting sick. If she's still feeling under the weather, would you mind popping in before you head to the hospital? I could rustle up a loaf of pumpkin bread for you to sweeten the deal."

Christopher grinned. "Sold."

Her eyes twinkling, Edith waved him to a chair. "Give me one minute while I ring her."

The minute stretched to five, and when Edith returned with a plastic-wrapped loaf of pumpkin bread in hand, her face was etched with concern.

"She sounds terrible. But she said asking you to stop by is too much of an imposition and not to bother."

"As you pointed out, I'm here anyway. It's no bother." Christopher picked up his bag from the chair in Edith's foyer.

"I couldn't convince her of that. But between you and me, I suspect her reluctance is more related to finances than inconvenience. According to J.C., she's been pinching pennies to put herself through school. Plus, she may not have much, if any, insurance."

"I'm running a special today. Buy one house call, get one free." He winked at Edith. "At least that will be my story when I show up at her door. What's her name?"

"Marci Clay." Edith twisted the knob and stepped aside to allow him to pass. "She's a very nice person. Pretty, too. I'm surprised she's not married."

An odd nuance in Edith's inflection put Christopher on alert, but when he paused on the porch and turned, her expression was guileless. Must have been his imagination.

"Call me if you have any more concerns about Maddie."

"I'll do that. But at the moment, I'm more worried about Marci."

"I'll check her out."

A tiny smile tugged at the corners of Edith's mouth as she handed him the pumpkin bread. "Sounds like a plan. Enjoy the treat."

She closed the door with a soft click—but not before he caught a suspicious gleam in her eyes. And that was *not* his imagination.

But it didn't matter.

Because no matter how nice or how pretty Marci Clay was, he wasn't interested.

Maybe someday he'd test the waters of romance again. Maybe. But during his two years living on Nantucket, he'd steered clear of all eligible women. And he didn't intend to change course anytime in the near future.

No matter what Edith might be planning.

As the doorbell chimed for the third time, Marci groaned and rolled over.

Go away!

She wanted to shout out that order, but her throat hurt too much to talk, let alone yell. It felt as if someone had taken sandpaper to it. Besides, whoever was at the door probably wouldn't hear her from her second-floor bedroom even if she could holler at full volume.

She'd fallen back asleep immediately after Edith's phone call, so she had no clue how much time had elapsed. But based on the angle of the sun slanting through the sheer curtains, it was still early.

Too early for visitors.

Except this one didn't seem to realize that, she concluded wearily as the bell chimed again. Nor did her persistent caller appear to have any intention of going away.

With a resigned sigh, she swung her legs to the floor and snagged the ratty velour bathrobe that had wrapped her in its fleecy warmth and comforted her through many a cold, lonely Chicago evening. Shrugging into it, she shuffled down the hall on unsteady legs and took the stairs one at a time, clinging to the banister.

Whoever had parked a finger against the doorbell was going to get an earful, she resolved, gritting her teeth.

Flipping the deadbolt, she tugged on the door and opened her mouth, prepared to give her visitor a piece of her mind.

But the words died in her throat as she came face-to-face with a tall, thirtyish man holding a black bag.

It was the preppy guy from the restaurant. The one who'd given her the blatant perusal.

She shut her mouth and stared.

He stared back.

When the silence lengthened, he cleared his throat. "Marci Clay?"

She gave a tiny nod.

"I'm Christopher Morgan. Edith called about me stopping by to…uh…check you out." His face grew ruddy, and his Adam's apple bobbed. "She said you weren't feeling well."

The guy who'd ogled her legs was the doctor Edith had offered to send over? A shiver rippled through Marci, and she edged back.

"I'm okay." She tightened her grip on the door

and started to ease it closed. No way did she want this jerk anywhere near her.

"You don't look okay."

Given how she felt, she figured that was the understatement of the century.

"I asked Edith to tell you not to bother." The words scraped painfully against her raw throat.

"And I told her this was your lucky day. Two house calls for the price of one." The ghost of a grin tugged at his lips. "You can't pass up a bargain like that."

She gave him a suspicious look. "No one does house calls anymore. Especially for free."

"I do. On occasion." He examined her flushed face. "What's your temperature?"

She lifted one shoulder. "I haven't looked for a thermometer yet."

"I could save you the trouble. I have a disposable one in my bag."

Marci studied the thin blue stripes on his white dress shirt as she debated her next move. She wasn't keen about getting up close and personal with this guy, but if she wanted to fulfill her obligations at The Devon Rose she needed medical attention. And in light of her shaky finances and bare-bones health insurance, free sounded awfully good.

"Look…about Saturday night. I'm sorry I stared."

Surprised he'd broached that subject—and taken

aback by the apologetic tone in his baritone voice—
she lifted her chin. And noticed several things she'd
missed on Saturday. Eyes as blue as the Nantucket
sea on a sunny day. Shoulders that looked broad
enough to carry the heaviest of loads. A firm chin
that conveyed strength and resolve. Light brown
hair sprinkled with the merest hint of silver at the
temples. And fine lines radiating from the corners
of his eyes that spoke of caring and compassion.

Her attitude toward him softened a fraction.

"I want you to know I'm not generally that rude."
His gaze held hers, steady and sincere. "My mother
raised me to treat women with respect, and I didn't
do that Saturday night. Please forgive me."

Was this guy for real? Marci scrutinized him for
any sign of deceit, any indication that this was a
standard line. And she'd heard plenty of those in her
life. But unless this guy was a world-class actor, he
meant what he'd said. He truly was sorry. And he
hadn't been too proud or arrogant or conceited to
admit his mistake.

In other words, he was a gentleman.

Not a species she'd often run across in her world.

The question was, how did one deal with a man
like this? She was far more used to tossing sassy
comebacks at guys who flirted with her at Ronnie's,
where she often spent as much of her shift deflecting advances as she did taking orders and deliver-
ing food, than she was to accepting apologies from
gentlemen.

"It's okay."

"No, it's not. So why not let me make amends? I can check out your temperature, get a little history, maybe figure out what's wrong. Edith tells me you're planning to manage The Devon Rose for the next couple of weeks, and it's obvious you're in no shape to do that right now. Helping get you back on your feet is the least I can do after my faux pas on Saturday."

Interesting how he'd positioned his assistance as a favor to *him,* Marci mused, leaning against the edge of the door as a sudden weariness swept over her. His offer sounded good, but there had to be a catch. There always was.

The man's eyes narrowed, and instead of waiting for her to respond, he stepped in. Literally. Taking her arm in a firm but gentle grip, he edged her back into the spacious foyer, shut the door with his shoulder and led her to a straight chair beside the steps.

"Where can I wash my hands?"

She motioned toward the restroom in what had once been the butler's pantry, unwilling to irritate her throat by speaking.

As he strode across the hardwood floor and disappeared through the dining room archway, she let her head drop back against the wall beneath the stairs that wound to the second floor. In general, high-handed men riled her. Yet despite his take-charge manner, Christopher Morgan came across as caring and competent rather than autocratic. Besides, she couldn't afford to take offense. She needed to get well, and it would be foolish to pass up free medical help.

But if he pulled out a stethoscope and aimed for her chest, she intended to smack him.

Talk about weird coincidences.

As Christopher washed his hands, drying them on one of the disposable guest towels beside the sink in the rest room, he wondered what the odds were of crossing paths again with the woman in the restaurant.

They had to be minuscule.

Unless more than chance was involved.

So often in the past, occurrences he'd written off as coincidence had turned out, in retrospect, to be part of God's plan for him. This could be one of them. Perhaps it was best to put the situation in the Lord's hands.

As he approached the foyer, his shoes silent on the large Chinese area rug in the dining room, he saw that Marci's head was resting against the wall, exposing the slender, delicate column of her throat. Her eyes were closed, the curve of her long lashes sweeping her cheeks in a graceful arc.

His step faltered. On Saturday, he'd been distracted by her great figure and fabulous legs, but today they were camouflaged by a worn, faded pink robe that covered her neck to toes—and directed his attention to her face. Her halo of blond hair softened a chin that was a tad too sharp, while well-defined cheekbones gave her features a slight angular appearance, adding a dash of character that kept her from being just another Kewpie-doll blonde. Full, appealing lips completed the picture.

In other words, Marci Clay was the kind of woman who would catch any man's eye.

But perhaps not for the right reasons, Christopher acknowledged. And her reaction to his appreciative perusal Saturday night indicated she knew that.

Her eyelids fluttered open, propelling him forward. If she caught him staring again, he suspected she'd hustle him out the door faster than a sand crab could scuttle back to its hole.

That suspicion was confirmed by the wariness in her deep green irises as he approached. While he couldn't help noticing the flecks of gold that sparked in their depths as he pulled up a chair beside her, he did his best to ignore them.

Snapping on a pair of latex gloves, he withdrew a disposable thermometer from his bag and tore off the wrapping. "Open up. We'll have a reading in sixty seconds."

He slid it under her tongue, and as they waited he took her wrist to check her pulse. Strong, if a bit fast. No problem there. He was more concerned about the subtle tremors beneath his fingertips. They could be due to weakness. More likely, though, they were fever-related chills. From the heat seeping through his glove, he knew he wasn't going to like her temperature.

Withdrawing the thermometer, he checked the reading. The number didn't surprise him. "A hundred and two."

She grimaced.

After slipping the thermometer into a small waste bag, he gave her his full attention. "Any idea what's going on?"

She shook her head.

"When did this start?"

"Yesterday."

"Anything hurt?"

"Throat."

"Any other symptoms?"

Again she shook her head.

Withdrawing a tongue depressor and penlight from his bag, he scooted closer to her. "Let's have a look."

As she opened her mouth, he inserted the tongue depressor and flashed the light to the back of her throat. Swelling and severe inflammation. Depositing the depressor in the waste bag, he reached over to gently feel the lymph nodes in her neck. Puffy.

She winced and tried to pull away. "Hurts."

"Sorry." He let her go and leaned back. "I think we may be dealing with a case of strep throat."

She squeezed her eyes shut, and he watched her lashes grow spiky with moisture.

"Hey, it's not the end of the world." To his surprise, the reassurance came out soft and husky. He cleared his throat. "You'll be back on your feet in a few days with the right care."

"I don't have a few days." She opened her eyes, blinking away the tears as she rasped out the shaky words.

He heard the panic in her voice and knew she was thinking about her duties at The Devon Rose.

"We'll get you well as fast as we can, okay?"

"Wednesday?"

He'd have liked to say yes, but he couldn't lie. "I doubt it."

"When?"

"Why don't we verify the strep diagnosis first?" Once more he turned to his bag, pulling out a small kit. "This is a rapid strep test. It will give us an answer in a few minutes. I see quite a few pediatric patients in my family practice, so I always have one of these with me. They come in handy, especially for the younger set. Not that you're over the hill, by any means." He smiled, trying to put her at ease as he set up the test.

The ploy didn't work. She eyed his preparations and gestured toward the kit. "How much?"

It took a moment for him to grasp that she was

asking the price of the test. As Edith had implied, money must be tight.

"I get free samples all the time. I try to pass that benefit on to my patients." While that was true, this kit wasn't a freebie. But she didn't have to know that.

Without giving her a chance to pursue the subject, he instructed her to open her mouth again and proceeded to swipe her throat with a long cotton swab. When he finished, he dipped the swab in a solution and placed a few drops on a test strip.

"While we wait for the results, let's assume it's strep and talk about treatment." He peeled off his gloves and dropped them into the waste bag. "Do you have any medicine allergies?"

She shook her head.

"Good. Let's go with penicillin." He started to pull a prescription pad out of his pocket.

"Won't this…" She stopped. Swallowed. Winced. "Won't this go away by itself?"

The money thing again, he realized.

"Yes. Usually in three to seven days." Leaving the prescription pad in his pocket, he crossed his arms over his chest.

"Maybe I'll get lucky, and it will be gone in three days." She pulled her robe tighter as a shiver rippled through her.

"Maybe. But antibiotics shorten the time you're contagious."

"By how much?"

"Most people stop being contagious twenty-four to forty-eight hours after they begin treatment. Without the pills, you could pass germs for two to three weeks, even if your symptoms go away. Not the best scenario in a restaurant."

As he checked the test strip, he tried to think of a diplomatic way to offer further assistance. Flipping it toward her, he indicated the test window. "Positive."

She groaned, and her expression grew bleak.

Dropping the strip into the waste bag, he sealed the top. "I'll tell you what. I've got a few samples of penicillin that will get you started." He removed a packet of four pills from his bag and handed them to her. "On my way back from the hospital later, I'll swing by my office and raid the sample closet. I think I can come up with enough to see you through. That way you won't have to run out to a pharmacy to get a prescription filled and spread germs all over town. I wouldn't want to be responsible for creating a public-health menace." He tried another grin.

It didn't work.

Marci fingered the sample packet, her manner once more wary. "I'm not in the habit of accepting favors."

At her suspicious look, he concluded that other men who'd done favors for her had expected a payback.

The thought sickened him.

"No strings attached, okay?" He held her gaze for a long moment, willing her to believe that not all men were crass or untrustworthy.

She searched his eyes, and after a few seconds he detected an almost imperceptible softening in her features.

"Do you have any over-the-counter medicine in the house that will help with the fever? Aspirin, ibuprofen?" Picking up his bag, he rose.

She looked up at him from beneath those impossibly long lashes and nodded.

"Take them on a regular basis. Drink lots of water. Rest. I'll leave the samples hanging on your doorknob after my shift in the E.R. That way I won't disturb you if you're resting."

He headed toward the door, and she trailed behind him. Pausing on the threshold, he withdrew a card from his pocket and handed it to her. "If you feel worse, or things don't improve by tomorrow, call me."

A few seconds ticked by as she read the card. Blinked. Swallowed. Lifting her chin, she looked into his eyes. "Thank you."

The expression of gratitude was delivered in a soft, shy tone that revealed an unexpected—and touching—vulnerability.

On Saturday night, he'd been drawn to her physical appearance. But right now he found her appealing in a different way. Although she was a little thing—a good eight or nine inches shorter than his six-foot frame, he estimated—she radiated a quiet strength and dignity that he sensed had been hard-earned. Marci Clay, he suspected was a survivor.

Yet that didn't jibe with the air of defeat and distress he'd picked up from her on Saturday.

So perhaps he was misjudging her character—as he'd misjudged Denise's.

That was a sobering thought.

Easing back a step, he gave her a brief, professional smile. "No problem. This is what being a doctor is supposed to be about. Now get some rest and take your medicine. You should feel much better by tomorrow. And if all goes well, I expect you can be back on the job by Thursday."

Without waiting for her to respond, he descended the porch steps and strode toward Edith's house, where he'd left his car.

As he set his bag on the backseat, he glanced toward The Devon Rose. The door was closed, but he detected a movement behind the lace curtain that screened the drawing room from the scrutiny of passersby. Had Marci been watching him?

The possibility pleased him—for reasons he didn't care to examine.

Sliding into the driver's seat, he sent a quick look toward Edith's house. And noticed the same phenomenon: a movement behind the sheer curtains at her living-room window. Had the older woman been observing him, too?

Considering the gleam he'd noticed earlier in her eyes, that notion *didn't* please him. On the contrary, it made him uncomfortable.

Edith Shaw was gaining a reputation as a matchmaker, thanks to her part in pairing two couples in the past two years. And he did *not* want to be her next victim.

Even if she had her sights set on a match as lovely as Marci Clay.

Chapter Two

"The Devon Rose."

"Marci? It's J.C."

"J.C.!" Setting aside a measuring cup, Marci tucked the phone closer to her ear and gave her brother her full attention. "How's Paris?"

"Romantic."

She grinned. "I'll bet. And how's Heather?"

"Happy. Gorgeous. Irresistible."

A female giggle sounded in the background, followed by a chuckle from J.C. Marci smiled. It was good to hear her big brother sounding lighthearted. He'd had more than enough worry to last a lifetime.

"Tell her I said hi."

"Will do. How's everything going?"

"Good. I'm whipping up a batch of scones from her recipe as we speak."

No way did Marci intend to tell them she'd been

sick. They deserved a carefree honeymoon. Besides, the penicillin had vanquished the strep throat in less than forty-eight hours. While she hadn't yet regained full strength, Christopher Morgan's prediction that she'd be back on the job by Thursday appeared to be coming true. She'd let Edith and Julie handle the tearoom today, but now that the last of their Wednesday guests had departed, she felt well enough to do a little baking.

"I told Heather you'd breeze through. But you know how to reach us if you need us."

"Your itinerary and contact numbers are taped to the fridge. I check them every morning so I can live your European tour vicariously. That's probably the closest I'll ever get to the real thing." She tried for a teasing tone, but couldn't quite pull it off. The truth of the statement was too depressing.

"Hey, your turn will come."

She tried again to lighten her tone. "Anything is possible, right?"

"With God."

At his quiet response, she stopped pretending. Looking out the window, she watched a bird take flight and aim for the sky. "He and I aren't well-acquainted."

"You could be."

"You never give up, do you?"

"No. And look how my persistence paid off with Nathan."

"That was different. Trust me. I'm a lost cause." The swinging door from the dining room opened as Edith bustled through with a tray, and Marci used that as an excuse to change the subject. "Look, we're in cleanup mode here, so I need to get back to work. Besides, I'm sure you have better things to do on your honeymoon than talk to your sister."

Is that J.C.? Edith mouthed, her eyes lighting up. Heather nodded.

"Tell him I said hi," she whispered. "Heather, too."

"Edith says hi to you both."

J.C. chuckled. "I'll pass that on. Call us if you need us."

"I will. Don't worry about anything here. You just have fun."

"We intend to. Talk to you soon."

As the line went dead, Marci set the portable phone back in its holder on the counter and picked up the measuring cup.

Edith planted her hands on her hips. "Don't I get a report?"

"I didn't ask for details." Marci filled the cup with flour and leveled it off. "But I got the impression they're enjoying themselves. And J.C. sounds happy."

The older woman's lips curved into a satisfied smile. "Excellent. I knew those two were meant for each other from day one. But getting them to see that took a bit of work."

From Heather, Marci had heard all about Edith's penchant for matchmaking. Although The Devon Rose proprietress claimed her neighbor's efforts hadn't had that much impact on her relationship with J.C., it was obvious Edith felt otherwise. Why disillusion her?

"All I know is I'm grateful their paths crossed. I'd given up on J.C. ever finding a wife."

"It was just a matter of meeting the right woman. Or, in Heather's case, the right man." Edith began empting the tray. "And speaking of men…is there some handsome man pining away for you back in Chicago?"

Only if you counted Ronnie at the diner, Marci thought as she dumped the flour into a mixing bowl. And by no stretch of the imagination could the fifty-something cook with the receding hairline and prominent paunch be called handsome.

"No. Men are more trouble than they're worth."

Edith shot her a startled glance. "Goodness. That's exactly what Heather used to say. Until J.C. came along, that is." The older woman picked up the empty tray and headed back toward the dining room, pausing on the threshold. "By the way, I saw Christopher Morgan at a meeting at church last night. He asked how you were doing. He's single, you know."

With a wink, Edith pushed through the swinging door and disappeared.

Flummoxed by both the comment and the unexpected little tingle that raced up her spine, Marci stared after her. Was Edith hinting that the doctor was interested in her? That the two of them…

No. She cut off that line of thought. It was preposterous. They knew nothing about each other. Meaning that if the man *was* interested in her, it was for the wrong reasons. And hormones were no basis for a relationship. She'd been there, done that. Repeating the experience held no appeal.

Yet…she did owe him a thank-you for his visit on Monday. Without his intervention, she'd probably still be out of commission. Somehow a note didn't seem sufficient. Perhaps she could offer a small token of appreciation?

As she stirred the dough, she mulled over the problem. What was an appropriate gift for a man? Most men didn't appreciate flowers. A CD would be okay, except she didn't know his taste in music.

Gathering the dough together with a few quick kneads, she dropped it onto the floured counter. And as she began rolling and cutting out the scones, the ideal solution came to her: food. What man didn't like home-cooked food? Bachelors, in particular. She had a killer recipe for chocolate-chip-pecan cookies.

Or better yet, why not send him a gift certificate for the tea room? He could even bring a date if he wanted to. Perfect.

Placing the scones on a baking sheet, she slid them into the oven as Edith returned to the kitchen.

"Julie's almost finished refilling the sugar bowls." The older woman set another tray of plates on the counter and moved toward the refrigerator. "I'll work on the jam and clotted cream for tomorrow. Another full house, according to the reservation book."

Casting a speculative look at Edith, Marci considered asking her if she knew Christopher Morgan's home address. According to Heather, the older woman was well-connected on the island. Even though she and Chester weren't natives, they'd embraced island life after their move to Nantucket a dozen years ago following Chester's retirement.

But she quickly nixed that notion. In light of Edith's implication that the man was interested in her, she didn't want to encourage any romantic plans her neighbor might be concocting. Especially since the Lighthouse Lane matriarch would have plenty of time and opportunity to implement them. Marci did *not* want to be dodging matchmaking attempts while living in the cottage behind Edith's house during her month-long vacation—J.C.'s graduation present to her.

It would be far safer to find the good doctor's address on her own.

Leaning his bike against the wall of his tiny 'Sconset cottage, Christopher shuffled through his mail as he walked to the back door, feet crunching on the oyster-shell path. Bill, bill, ad, postcard from Bermuda—he flipped it over and read the message from his brother, grinning at his seven-year-old nephew's scrawled signature that took up half the writing area.

"Hey, there, Christopher."

Looking up, he smiled at his elderly landlord on the other side of the picket fence that separated the yards of their adjoining cottages, which backed to the sea.

"Hi, Henry. What's up?" He strolled over, giving his neighbor a swift assessment.

"Now, you put away those doctor eyes of yours." The man shook a finger at him. "Don't be sizing me up every time we talk just because I had a bout of pneumonia last winter. I hope you're as resilient as I am at eighty-four."

A chuckle rumbled in Christopher's chest. "I do, too." In the past two years, since Christopher had rented Henry's second, tiny cottage, the older man had bounced back from the few ailments he'd experienced.

"Any good mail?"

At Henry's question, Christopher began riffling through the letters again. "Mostly bills and ads. But I did get a postcard from my brother." He handed it over.

Pulling a pair of wire-rimmed glasses out of his

shirt pocket, Henry examined the photo of the expansive beach. "Pretty, isn't it? Always wanted to see that pink sand." He handed it back.

"Would you still like to go?"

"Nope. Did plenty of gallivanting in my army days. I'm happy to be an armchair traveler now. Don't have to worry about terrorists on airplanes or fighting crowds or losing luggage. You can't beat the Travel Channel." He leaned closer to Christopher and peered at one of the envelopes in his hand. "That looks interesting."

Christopher checked out the return address. The Devon Rose. That *was* interesting.

Slitting the envelope, he pulled out a single sheet of paper folded in half. Inside he found a gift certificate and a short note written in a scrawling hand.

Dr. Morgan:
Thank you for your assistance on Monday. The penicillin took care of the problem. Please enjoy tea for two as a token of my appreciation.

It was signed by Marci Clay.

It would be difficult to imagine a more impersonal message. Yet Christopher's heart warmed as he ran a finger over the words inked by Marci's hand.

"Maybe interesting wasn't the right word."

As Henry's eyes narrowed in speculation, heat crept up Christopher's neck. "It's a gift certificate. I did an impromptu house call a few days ago, and the patient was grateful. You ever been here?" He waved the envelope at Henry, hoping to distract him.

It didn't work.

"Female patient?"

The man might be old, but he was still sharp, Christopher conceded. And if he tried to dodge the question, Henry would get more suspicious. "Yes. Her brother just married the owner, and she's running the place while they're on their honeymoon. Hence the invitation." Christopher paused as an idea took shape. "Don't you have a birthday coming up?"

"I stopped counting those long ago."

"June eighth." Christopher had jotted the occasion on his calendar. Henry might pretend not to care about his birthday, but he'd been thrilled last year when his tenant had treated him to an upscale dinner at The Chanticleer. "How about you and I give this a try on your big day?" He held up the gift certificate.

Sliding his palms into the back pockets of his slacks, Henry bowed forward like a reed, his knobby elbows akimbo, his expression dubious. "Kind of fancy-schmancy, isn't it?"

"You deserve fancy on your birthday."

"You ought to take some pretty little lady to a place like that."

An image of Marci flashed through his mind, but Christopher pushed it aside. "Pretty little ladies seem to be in short supply these days."

"You're not looking in the right places, then."

"I'm not looking, period."

"I know." Henry sighed. "But you've got to move on, Christopher. You can't let one bad experience ruin your life. I learned that after Korea. Lots of the guys in my outfit couldn't get past the bad stuff once they came home. Haunted them for the rest of their lives. I wouldn't want that to happen to you. You're thirty-six years old. You should have a wife and a bunch of kids by now."

"I'll get around to that one of these days."

"You said that last year."

Christopher laid a hand on the older man's bony shoulder. "I appreciate your concern, Henry. But this is best for now." He lifted the certificate again. "In the meantime, do we have a date?"

The man grinned. "I expect we do. Shall I break out my tie?"

"I will if you will."

"It's a deal."

As Marci returned from showing two guests to their table, a tall man with deep blue eyes, dressed in khaki slacks and a navy blue blazer, stepped into the foyer of The Devon Rose.

Christopher Morgan.

He smiled when he saw her, the fine fan of lines at the corners of his eyes crinkling. "You're looking a lot better."

A disconcerting ripple of warmth spread through her as he drew close, and she wiped her palms down her slim black skirt. "I'm *feeling* a lot better."

"That's good news." He held up a familiar piece of paper. "I'm here to redeem my gift certificate."

Julie must have taken the reservation, Marci concluded, skimming the names on the day's seating chart. There it was. Morgan. Table six. For two.

He'd brought a date.

Her warm feeling evaporated.

Steeling herself, she looked up again, expecting to see some gorgeous female lurking behind him.

Instead, a wiry, wizened old man with thin, neatly combed gray hair popped out and grinned at her. But he directed his question to Christopher.

"Is this the lady who sent you the certificate?"

"She's the one."

Henry's grin broadened as he inspected Marci. "It's my birthday. Eighty-five years and counting."

"Wow! That does deserve a celebration." Marci smiled back.

"At my age, every day I wake up is worth celebrating." His eyes twinkled as he stuck out his hand. "Name's Henry Calhoun. I'm Christopher's neighbor. Nice to meet you."

She returned his firm shake. "Marci Clay."

"Nice place you have here." He perused the foyer and grand staircase. "My wife came here once, years ago. Had a great time, as I recall."

"We'll do our best to see that you do, too."

The front door opened again, admitting more patrons, and Christopher turned to his companion. "We'd better let Ms. Clay show us to our table, Henry."

"Maybe she can stop by and chat with us again later." The older man gave her a hopeful look.

"I'd be happy to."

She led the way to their corner table in one of the twin parlors, offering them a tea menu. "Julie will be back in a few minutes to answer any questions and take your tea order. Enjoy the experience."

"We will," Henry assured her. "I even wore a tie for the occasion." He flapped the out-of-date accessory at her.

Marci did her best to stifle a grin. Based on width alone, the tie had to be at least twenty years old. "You look very spiffy."

"Spiffy?" Christopher's mouth tipped up in amusement, distracting her. He had nice lips, she noted.

Jolted by that observation, she summoned up a frown to counter it. "What's wrong with spiffy?"

"Nothing. It's just a rather old-fashioned term."

"Maybe she's an old-fashioned girl," Henry chimed in. "And if you ask me, no one's ever come up with a better compliment than spiffy. Thank you, my dear."

"You're very welcome. I'll be back a little later to see how you enjoyed the tea."

Returning to the foyer, Marci continued to seat the guests, mindful of the pair of men at the corner table every time she entered the sitting room. Once the tea got underway, however, she worked a wedding shower in the dining room while Julie handled the twin sitting rooms on the other side of the foyer.

But—much to her annoyance—her thoughts kept straying to the blue-eyed doctor. And each time they did, her fingers grew clumsy. She dropped a silver server on the floor. Sloshed some hot water on the white linen as she set down a fresh teapot. Knocked over the sugar bowl, sending cubes tumbling across the starched tablecloth.

She tried to blame her fumblings on a simple physical awareness of the man's striking good looks, but she knew it went deeper than that. Since his faux pas in the restaurant, he'd been a total gentleman. It didn't seem fair to hold a brief lapse against him. He wasn't the first man to notice her legs. Or her body. Nor would he be the last. But he *was* the first to apologize for his rude behavior.

And that made him special.

Who was he, really? Marci wondered, peeking over her shoulder as she lifted the lid on the tea chest so the bride-to-be could make her selection.

She could just catch a glimpse of his strong profile as he spoke with Henry, the fragile bone china teacup looking child-size in his long, lean fingers. Had he been born on Nantucket? Where did he live? What did he do in his free time?

Did he have a girlfriend?

But none of those questions mattered, she reminded herself, turning back to the bride-to-be. Least of all the last one. She wasn't going to be on Nantucket long enough to get to know anyone. She was here to rest and relax after seven grueling years of school and work. Then she'd begin her job search and build a future for herself that didn't include slinging hash at Ronnie's. Or relying on others to validate her.

She'd done that once, and it had been a huge mistake. One she didn't intend to repeat. Going forward, only the two men she trusted to love her for the right reasons would be granted access to her heart: her brothers, J.C. and Nathan.

Yet as she closed the tea chest and took one more wistful glance across the room toward the tall, handsome man juggling a teacup, she found herself wishing there could be an exception to that rule.

Even though she knew such romantic fancies were only the stuff of fairy tales.

"Now that was a mighty tasty birthday feast." Henry wiped his mouth on the linen napkin and leaned back in his chair, nursing a final cup of tea.

"I second that." Christopher slathered his last miniscone with generous layers of wild strawberry jam and imported clotted cream. "Not so good for the cholesterol, though."

"I'm eighty-five. If cholesterol hasn't gotten me yet, I doubt it will. And if it does—" he gestured to his empty plate "—what a way to go."

Christopher consumed the scone in one bite and chuckled. "It's hard to argue with that."

Scanning the room, Henry folded his napkin and set it beside his plate. "I hope Marci remembers to stop by. She's a nice girl."

"Seems to be."

"She's not wearing a ring."

Uh-oh. Christopher knew where this was heading.

"She's also only here for a short time, Henry."

"Doesn't take long."

"For what?"

"To know if someone's a good match." A soft smile tugged at the older man's lips. "When I met Marjorie at that USO dance, things clicked right away. I won't say it was love at first sight, but I knew the potential was there. We were married for fifty-four years, so I guess my instincts weren't too shabby."

Christopher swallowed. "Not everyone is blessed with sound instincts."

"You were. Otherwise you wouldn't be such a good doctor."

He gave a slight shrug. "Then I guess they don't translate to my personal life."

"What happened with Denise wasn't your fault, Christopher. The problem was her, not you."

Brushing a few crumbs into a neat pile on the snowy linen, Christopher picked them up and deposited them on his plate. When he'd come to Nantucket, he'd had no intention of sharing the story of his ill-fated romance with anyone. But he'd changed his mind one stormy night a few weeks into his stay after he'd discovered his landlord trying to batten down the gazebo his late wife had cherished.

Though Christopher had pitched in, they'd been unable to stop the brutal wind from ripping it apart and hurling pieces of it down the beach. Christopher had wrapped a protective arm around the older man's shoulders and guided him inside, to safety. But he hadn't been able to pry Henry away from the window. As the older man had watched the storm destroy the gazebo, tears streaking down his cheeks, he'd told Christopher he'd built it for his beloved wife years ago. That it had become her favorite place. And that it was the only spot where he could still feel her presence.

Now it was gone.

Christopher had stayed to console Henry. But later, over strong cups of coffee and a stubby candle—the electricity had also been a victim of the storm—he'd found their roles reversed when Henry asked him about his own life and what had brought him to Nantucket. As the wind howled and the world was reduced to the diameter of a candle flame, he'd opened his heart—and sealed their friendship.

In the ensuing months, Christopher had come to value the man's insights and advice. About everything except Denise.

"I'm not sure the problem was all hers, Henry. Besides, you didn't know her."

"I know you. That's enough."

Though he was gratified by his friend's loyalty, Christopher was far less certain where the blame lay.

"Well, gentlemen, how was your tea?"

They both looked up. Marci stood beside their table, a small white box in hand.

"Best tea I ever went to," Henry declared, beaming up at her.

Christopher quirked an eyebrow at him. As far as he knew, this was the *only* tea Henry had ever gone to.

The older man ignored his skeptical reaction. "What did you think, Christopher?"

"Very nice." He smiled at Marci, appreciating how the simple but elegant white silk blouse showed off her figure. "Thank you again for the invitation."

"It was the least I could do. I was in desperate straits the day you stopped by. The antibiotics worked magic." Transferring her attention to Henry, she set the small white box on the table. "Julie told me you were partial to the chocolate tarts, Mr. Calhoun. Here are a few more to take home so you can extend your birthday celebration."

He laid a gnarled hand on the box and gave her a pleased smile. "That's mighty sweet of you. And it's Henry, please. Now tell me, how are you enjoying Nantucket?"

"I'm afraid I haven't seen much yet. But I intend to make up for that as soon as my brother and sister-in-law get back."

"How long will you be staying?"

"I have five weeks left. One more to work, and four to play. I plan to take a month of vacation before I get serious about looking for a job. I just finished my master's."

"In what?"

"Social work."

"My, that's impressive."

"Hardly." She gave him a wry grin. "Most people my age are already well-established in their careers. I was a late bloomer."

Henry cocked his head. "Couldn't have been that late. You don't look more than twenty-four, twenty-five."

She chuckled. "Try thirty-one."

"Thirty-one." Henry shot his host a speculative look. "That's a perfect age."

The sudden gleam in Henry's eyes reminded Christopher of the one he'd seen in Edith's the day he'd made the house call. It was time to steer the conversation to a safer topic. Like sightseeing.

"It's nice that you'll have a chance to enjoy the island at leisure," he offered, keeping his tone conversational. "A lot of people only stay for a weekend, or make it a day trip. You'll be able to explore all the beaches. And be sure to visit the lighthouses."

"Especially Sankaty," Henry said, jumping back in. "That's real close to where I live, in 'Sconset." His expression grew thoughtful. "Tell you what. Why don't you ring me if you're out my way, and I can ride along and give you some history? I could take you on a tour of the Lifesaving Museum, too. I'm a trustee there. Then you could come back to my place and have some of my homemade banana-nut bread. It can't compare to these—" he tapped the box in front of him "—and I don't make it as well as my wife did, but I like to keep it on hand. I think of her whenever I have a slice." His voice choked, and he cleared his throat.

Marci's features softened, effecting a subtle, appealing transformation in her face that tugged at Christopher's heart. "I'd like that, Henry. And banana-nut bread is one of my favorites, too."

"It's a date, then." He extracted a pen and small scrap of paper from his jacket, speaking as he wrote. "Here's my phone number. You give me a call anytime."

"I'll do that." Marci slipped the piece of paper into the pocket of her skirt.

"Maybe I can convince Christopher to join us, if he's not working. He's partial to my banana-nut bread, too."

That suggestion seemed to fluster her, Christopher noted, still focused on her face. She took a small step back and clasped her hands in front of her. "Dr. Morgan is probably very busy, Henry. I'm on vacation. He's not."

"He works too hard. A little R & R would do him good. And you can call him Christopher. We don't stand on formality around here."

When Marci shot Christopher an uncertain glance, he cleared his throat and spoke up.

"Please do." He smiled, and as they stared at each other, his pulse tripped into double time.

It was Henry who finally broke the charged silence. "I think we're overstaying our welcome, Christopher." He gestured to the deserted tearoom, where Julie was beginning to clear tables. "These lovely ladies have work to do."

Dragging his gaze away from Marci, Christopher pushed back his chair—and willed the warmth creeping up his neck to stay below his collar. "Thanks again."

Marci gave him a stiff nod. "It was a pleasure. I'll call you, Henry."

"I'll look forward to it."

In silence, Christopher followed the older man to the front door, taking his arm as they descended the steps.

"She's a sweet girl," Henry offered.

"Yes, she is."

"Great legs, too."

A smile tugged at Christopher's lips. "Yeah, I noticed."

Henry grinned up at him. "That's the best news I've heard in a month of Sundays."

Christopher's smile faded, and he sent his landlord a stern look. "Don't get any ideas, Henry."

"I wasn't the one with ideas back there." His eyes twinkled. "I may be old, but I'm not blind. I saw the way you looked at her."

"She's a very pretty woman. But appreciating beauty isn't the same as pursuing it."

"True." Henry's grin widened. "But it's a start."

Shaking his head, Christopher opened the car door for his neighbor. Henry could be as tenacious as a Nantucket deer tick when he got a notion into his head. And he doubted there was anything he could say to dissuade the older man from his fanciful conclusions. The best he could do was avoid talking about Marci in Henry's presence.

Except he had a sneaking feeling Henry wasn't going to cooperate with that plan.

Chapter Three

"I feel bad about putting you to this expense, J.C."

Pushing through the gate in the tall privet hedge surrounding Edith's backyard, J.C. shot Marci a disgruntled look over his shoulder as she trailed along behind him. "We've been over this a dozen times. After seven years of nonstop work and school, you deserve a vacation to celebrate your graduation. Since you won't stay with Heather and me, this is a good alternative."

"I can't stay with you. You're newlyweds. But this doesn't feel right, either." Marci followed her brother down a flagstone path through the well-tended yard. Considering the high prices on the island, her big brother was probably spending a fortune on the month's rent for the little outbuilding that Chester had turned into a guest cottage.

Heaving a frustrated sigh, J.C. stopped, set Marci's

bags on a wooden bench and took her shoulders in a firm grasp. She had to tip her head back to look up into his dark eyes. "It's a gift, okay? All those years you worked long hours at the diner to support yourself while going to school, you wouldn't take a dime of help. None of the checks I sent you were ever cashed. I want to do this."

"I appreciate the gesture, J.C. And I'm grateful." She folded her arms across her chest. "But I don't need my own cottage. The youth hostel would be fine. This is too expensive."

His intent gaze locked on hers. "You're worth every penny."

That was the real problem, and they both knew it. While Marci's self-image had improved over the years, deep inside she still felt unworthy of such generosity and kindness.

When she didn't respond, J.C. shook his head. "I've never understood why you have such a hard time valuing yourself."

And he never would, not if she had anything to say about it, Marci vowed. With his law-enforcement background, he could have discovered the truth long ago. But when she'd dropped out of school at nineteen and hit the road, promising to stay in touch if he gave her space, he'd kept his word.

Five years later, when she told him she'd come home if he'd leave her past alone, he'd agreed. And he'd never reneged on that promise. Never used his resources as a police detective to invade her privacy. That's why she loved him—for his honor and integrity and unconditional love. He was the only person in her whole life she'd been able to count on, no matter what. The only person who had believed in her, who trusted in her basic goodness. She could never jeopardize his opinion of her by telling him the truth.

It wasn't worth the risk.

Hugging herself tighter, she shrugged. "I just think you have better uses for your money."

He continued to study her for a few moments, then released her shoulders and picked up her bags again. "If it makes you feel any better, Edith gave me a great deal. A bonus for my long tenure, as she put it. Most people only take island cottages for a week or two. I rented for a whole year—even during the quiet season, when she's normally closed. According to her, I was a bonanza." He grinned at her over his shoulder. "I've been called a lot of things in my life, but that was a new one."

As they approached the tiny clapboard cottage surrounded by budding hydrangea bushes, Marci stopped protesting. It wouldn't do any good, anyway. J.C. was determined to give her a month of fun, and obsessing over the cost would ruin the gift for both of them. For once in her life, she needed go with the flow.

Besides, J.C. had probably already paid the bill.

Setting the bags by the door, J.C. turned the knob, grinned and motioned her inside. "You're going to love this."

Easing past him, Marci stepped over the threshold—and froze. "Wow!"

J.C.'s grin broadened as he nudged her farther in with his shoulder and snagged her bags. "That's the reaction I was hoping for."

He edged around her as she took in the space she would call home for the next month. Though the structure was small, the vaulted ceiling and white walls gave it an unexpected feeling of spaciousness, and the blue-and-yellow color scheme created a cheery mood.

The compact unit was well-equipped, too, Marci noted. A queen-size bed stood in the far corner, while closer to the door a small couch upholstered in hydrangea-print fabric and an old chest that served as a coffee table formed a sitting area. To the right of the front door a wooden café-sized table for two was tucked beside a window in a tiny kitchenette.

The whole place looked like a display in a designer showroom.

In other words, it was a far cry from her tiny, decrepit apartment in Chicago, with its chipped avocado fixtures, burn-damaged Formica countertops and stained linoleum. The same apartment she'd be returning to in a month, when this magical sojourn was over.

"Did you notice the pumpkin bread?"

J.C.'s question distracted her from that depressing thought.

Looking in the direction he indicated, she noted the plastic-wrap-covered plate on the café table.

"Edith left some for me, too, my first day here. And trust me, there will be more. She'll take good care of you."

Marci shoved her hands in the pockets of her jeans. "I can take care of myself."

Shaking his head, J.C. pulled her into a bear hug. "What am I going to do with you?"

"Love me." The words came out muffled against his shirt as she hugged him back.

"Always."

Giving her one more squeeze, he stepped back. "Don't forget that Heather and I are taking you to dinner tomorrow." He held up his hand as she started to protest. "No arguments. You've been outvoted." A yawn caught him off guard, and he grinned. "The jet lag is catching up with me."

"Go home. You guys must be dead on your feet after flying all day. I need to settle in anyway."

"Okay. Want to join us for church tomorrow?"

She folded her arms across her chest and arched an eyebrow.

"Hey, you can't blame a guy for trying. We'll see you later, then. Sleep well."

As he exited and shut the door, Marci once more

surveyed her new digs. Though she still felt guilty about the expense, she couldn't stop the small smile that tugged at her lips. Maybe all this would disappear in a month, as Cinderella's coach had vanished at the stroke of midnight. But in the meantime, she felt like a princess. The only thing missing was the handsome prince.

An image of Christopher Morgan suddenly flashed through her mind. He certainly fit that description, she conceded. Tall. Handsome. Confident. Charming.

Looks and manners could be deceiving though. A practiced rake could hide a callous, selfish heart until he got what he wanted. And princes could turn out to be scoundrels—leaving broken hearts, shattered dreams and wrenching regrets in their wake.

Her instincts told her Christopher wasn't like that. But those same instincts had led her astray once.

And no way did she intend to trust them a second time.

Three days after the honeymooners returned—and two days into her vacation—Marci kept the promise she'd made to Henry two weeks before. After a morning spent soaking up rays on the beach, she'd headed for 'Sconset. True to his word, the older man had given her a tour of the area and invited her back to his home for refreshments.

"That was great banana-nut bread, Henry."

He topped off Marci's coffee mug as they sat on his back porch. "Glad you liked it."

"The tour was fabulous, too. I can't believe they actually moved Sankaty Light."

"Yep. It was quite a feat. Made the national news, even. Cost a bundle of money, but that was the only way to save it from tumbling into the sea, what with all the erosion over there. Moved it inch by inch. Slow and steady."

"Slow and steady is a good thing. With lighthouses—and life." Marci took a sip of her coffee as she gazed at the sea, separated from Henry's backyard by only a white picket fence and a stretch of beach.

"I expect that's true, most of the time. I know my Marjorie felt that way about her garden. She had the patience of Job with all these plants." Henry gestured toward the curving, overgrown flower beds that hugged much of the picket fence and porch, leaving only a small bit of lush green grass in the center and back of the yard.

"She tucked them into the ground, nurtured them, gave them time to flourish. Started most everything from seeds and cuttings. I often told her it would be a whole lot faster to buy established plants, but she claimed things grew better if they had a stable home from the beginning."

A sudden film of moisture clouded her vision,

and Marci blinked to clear it away. "Your wife was a wise woman." Sensing Henry's scrutiny, she shifted in her seat. She'd already learned that the older man was an astute observer; she didn't want him delving into her life. "Did she spend a lot of time in her garden?"

"Practically lived out here in the summer. Not that you'd know it now." He inspected the weed-choked beds and sighed. "I tried to keep up with things for the first few years after she died, not that I was ever much of a gardener. But arthritis finally did me in. Bending isn't as easy as it used to be. Makes me sad, how much it's deteriorated."

"How long has your wife been gone?"

"An eternity." He drew in a slow breath, then let it out. "Feels that long, anyway, after more than half a century of marriage. But to be exact, ten years and two months."

It was nice to know some relationships lasted, Marci reflected with a pang as she studied the garden in which Marjorie Calhoun had invested so much labor and love. Despite the neglect, hints of its former beauty remained. Here and there, hardy flowers poked through the rampant weeds. Although out-of-control ivy was attempting to choke a circle of hydrangeas in one corner, the bushes were sporting buds. And a climbing rose in desperate need of pruning competed for fence space with a tangle of morning-glory vines behind an oversized birdbath.

"What was over there, Henry?" Marci indicated the hydrangeas, which rimmed a spot bare except for some low-growing foliage she assumed was weeds.

"Used to be a gazebo. I built it for Marjorie years ago. She loved to sit out there with a glass of lemonade after she worked in the garden and enjoy the fruits of her labors. Lost it in a storm winter before last."

Marci rubbed a finger over the peeling white paint on the arm of her wicker rocker and mulled over all Henry had told her during their sightseeing outing. About Nantucket—and his life. He hadn't dwelt on his problems, focusing instead on all the good things he'd experienced in his eighty-five years.

But she'd learned about the bad, too, through offhand comments or in response to questions she'd asked. Henry had watched friends die in battle. Nursed his wife through a cancer scare. And now he struggled to maintain the life he loved as his vigor and strength ebbed and the cost of living on the island soared.

Long life, she supposed, was both a blessing and a curse.

As if he'd read her mind, Henry looked over at her, the afternoon sunlight highlighting the crevices on his face. "I'll tell you something, Marci. Growing old isn't for sissies."

Her throat constricted, and she leaned over to place a hand on his gnarled fingers. "Your body may be old, but your spirit is young. And I suspect it always will be."

He patted her hand. "Thank you, my dear."

Looking the garden over again, she set her empty mug aside and rose as an idea began to take shape in her mind. "Can you distinguish between the weeds and flowers, Henry?"

"Yes."

"Then why don't we clean this place up? You can point out the weeds until I learn which is which, and I can pull them up."

"But I didn't invite you here today to work."

She gave an impatient shrug. "I've worked my whole life. I can't just lie around on a beach every day for the next month. I'll go stir-crazy. I need to do something productive, too. This would be a challenge. And it would be fun." She scanned the garden again. "I bet we could whip this place into shape in no time."

"You might not think it's so much fun after you start getting blisters on your hands." He gave her a skeptical look. "Besides, gardening is hard work. It takes a lot of strength. Lifting, digging, pulling. You're just a little thing."

A wry smile lifted her lips. "Henry, I've spent half my life juggling heavy trays of dishes and glasses. I've moved tables, hauled and stacked chairs, and run up and down stairs balancing plates of food. At Ronnie's Diner, I'm known as the Bionic Blonde. Trust me, being a waitress is a tough job. I'm a whole lot stronger than I look."

"Well, I sure would like to see this place the way it used to be. And I know Marjorie would be pleased."

"Then it's decided. Heather and J.C. said I could use their car every afternoon, so I can bike to a beach and play in the sand in the morning, then head out here and play in the dirt after lunch. Are you game to show me the ropes?"

A slow grin creased his face, and he hauled himself out of his chair to stand beside her. "Let's do it."

Christopher wheeled his bike behind his cottage, glanced toward Henry's backyard—and came to an abrupt halt. He had only a partial view of the woman on her hands and knees between two hydrangea bushes, but he'd recognize that blond hair anywhere.

What in the world was Marci Clay doing in Henry's garden?

As she began to tug on something out of his line of sight, Henry's voice rang across the yards. "Hey, Christopher! Look what we're doing!"

Marci lost her grip and fell back with a plop. A second later she twisted toward him with a startled expression.

"Hi, Henry. Hello, Marci."

Scrambling to her feet, she wiped her hands on her jeans.

"We're cleaning out the garden," Henry told him, brandishing a shovel as he gestured toward a large pile of wilting weeds and ivy.

Setting his mail on the railing around his tiny back porch, Christopher strolled over to the picket fence that separated the yards and surveyed Henry's garden. In the far corner, plants had emerged from the cacophony of weeds. He'd never been much of a gardener, but his mother had enjoyed the hobby and he'd learned a few things from her. Enough to recognize the peony buds and coral bells. The other plants Marci had unearthed were a mystery to him.

"Looks like you've made a good start." He turned his attention to Marci, who'd kept her distance. Her jeans were grimy, her fingernails caked with mud. Sweat had wiped her face clean of makeup. One of her cheeks sported a long streak of dirt.

She looked adorable.

Ignoring the quickening of his pulse, Christopher summoned up what he hoped passed for a casual smile. "I see Henry put you to work."

"I volunteered."

"She's a hard worker, too." Henry rested the shovel against the fence. "Why are you home so early?"

Christopher checked his watch. "It's almost six-thirty."

"Six-thirty!" Shock rippled across Marci's face. "Henry, I've got to go. I told Edith and Chester I'd have dinner with them tonight. At seven." She rubbed her hands on her jeans again and dashed for the porch. "But I'll be back tomorrow."

"Are you still sure about doing this, Marci?"

"Yes." She grabbed her purse and rummaged through it. "I never leave a job unfinished." Snagging her keys, she sent Christopher a quick glance, tucked her hair behind her ear and looked away.

Why was she nervous around him? He didn't think it had anything to do with their rough start. Her present behavior bore no resemblance to her cold, aloof response when he'd insulted her in the restaurant. Today she reminded him of the island deer that bolted when anyone got too close.

For more than two years, he'd gone out of his way to discourage any woman who tried to cozy up to him. And a lot of them had. But Marci was at the opposite end of the spectrum. She was sending clear no-trespassing signals.

He should be grateful, Christopher told himself. This way he wouldn't have to worry about fending off unwanted attention.

Except he wasn't.

When the silence lengthened, Henry shot Christopher a pointed look. "Maybe you could walk Marci to her car."

"Oh, no, that's all right, Henry." Marci dropped her keys. Bent to pick them up. When she rose, her cheeks were flushed. "I'm right in front. He doesn't need to bother." Before either man could respond, she jogged toward the gate. "See you tomorrow, Henry."

Less than thirty seconds later, an engine started. Christopher heard the crunch of car tires on the oyster-shell lane and listened as the sound gradually receded into the distance.

When silence descended, he regarded Henry, gesturing toward the garden. "How did all this start?"

His neighbor scratched his head. "Beats me. One minute we were talking about Marjorie, and the next thing I knew Marci was pulling weeds. She's strong, too, just like she told me. Claims it comes from all those years of waitressing."

"Marci was a waitress?"

"Yep. That's how she put herself through school. You've got to admire her spunk."

"What else did she tell you?" Though Christopher did his best to keep his question nonchalant, a twinkle appeared in Henry's eyes.

"Mostly we talked about flowers. But I expect we'll get into a lot of other things as we work on the garden. Maybe you could stop by one afternoon and join us for lemonade."

Not a good idea, Christopher decided. Contact could lead to connection, and he wasn't in the market for a romantic relationship—even if the woman was willing. And Marci obviously wasn't.

Besides, he couldn't erase the image of her tears that first night in the restaurant. Or the defeated look in her eyes. Or the dejected slump of her shoulders as she'd walked home. All of which told him she had issues.

He needed to keep his distance.

"She makes you nervous, doesn't she?"

At Henry's comment, Christopher frowned. The last thing he needed right now was an armchair psychologist analyzing him in his backyard.

Ignoring Henry's remark, Christopher scanned the sky as a gust of wind whipped past. "Looks like a storm might be brewing."

His neighbor stacked his hands on top of the handle of his shovel and squinted at Christopher appraisingly. "Yep. I'd say there could be some unsettled weather ahead."

Disregarding the double meaning, Christopher motioned toward his porch. "I think I'll rescue my mail and head inside."

Henry grinned. "Dashing for cover, hmm? Good luck." With a wave, he ambled back to his hydrangeas.

For a minute, Christopher watched as the older man putzed around among the bushes. It was clear Henry thought he was running scared. And truth be told, he was. Marci was way too appealing.

But if Henry and Edith thought they were going to match him up with the attractive blonde, they'd be disappointed.

No way was he ready to get serious about anyone. Especially a woman whose eyes held secrets.

Chapter Four

Marci cast a wary eye at the clouds massing on the horizon as she drove down Milestone Road toward Henry's house on Wednesday. They'd begun to gather while she'd lounged on the beach this morning, and they'd grown more ominous during her brief stop at her cottage to grab some lunch and change into work clothes. If they continued to build, she suspected her gardening efforts would be curtailed this afternoon.

For now, though, the sun continued to shine brightly on the windswept moors and cranberry bog to her left. Already this long stretch of undulating road was becoming one of her favorite spots. Far less populated than other parts of the island, the pristine beauty and serenity of the simple, timeless landscape helped calm her. And she needed some calming—thanks to a certain good-looking doctor with eyes the color of a Nantucket sky.

Marci had no idea why—or how—he'd managed to get under her skin and disrupt her equilibrium in such a short time. And the first glance they'd exchanged in the restaurant had been anything but tender or romantic.

Yet from the day he'd apologized when he'd made the house call at The Devon Rose, she'd had difficulty controlling the attraction she felt whenever she was in his presence.

Or *thought* about being in his presence.

Like now.

Forcibly redirecting her attention to the bike path that followed the road toward 'Sconset, she saw that the cyclists were out in force today. Family groups for the most part, with a few couples here and there.

She did spot one solitary biker up ahead, though, on the outskirts of the village. A man in jeans, the wire baskets on the back of his bike loaded down. With what? she wondered. Paraphernalia for a beach outing? Picnic food? And why was he alone?

As Marci passed him, she caught a glimpse of his profile. And her mouth dropped open.

It was Christopher Morgan.

Yanking her gaze away from him, she pressed on the accelerator. Not until she'd put some distance between them did she risk another peek at him in her rearview mirror.

What in the world was he doing on a bicycle?

Didn't doctors usually drive luxury cars? And why wasn't he working on a weekday?

With those questions echoing in her mind, Marci navigated the narrow streets of the tiny village and pulled to a stop in front of Henry's cottage. For several seconds she sat there, engine running. She'd planned to be long gone by the time Christopher arrived home. Now, the only way to avoid another unsettling encounter with him would be to put the car back in gear, drive away and call Henry with her regrets. She hated to disappoint the older man, but that seemed the safest course.

Before she could follow through with that plan, however, Henry's front door opened. Pushing through, he strolled over to the car and leaned down to peer in the open passenger-side window.

"Thought I heard a car stop. Everything okay?"

Too late for retreat.

"Yes." Resigned, Marci shut off the engine, picked up her purse and opened her door just as Christopher rounded the corner on his bike.

"Hey, Christopher!" Henry straightened up and waved as he called out the greeting.

Christopher raised one hand in response.

Circling the car, Marci stood behind Henry. "What's he doing on a bike?"

"Always rides it to work in good weather. Sometimes in not-so-good weather. Says it helps keep him in shape."

Noting Christopher's toned, fit form as he pedaled toward them, Marci couldn't argue with that. Nor could she stop the slight quiver in her fingers as she took in his lean physique.

Get a grip! she warned herself, shoving her hands into her pockets and balling them into fists.

"So what's he doing home on a weekday?" She strove for a conversational tone but couldn't hide the tremor in her voice.

"He only has office hours until noon on Wednesdays. Then he works three to eleven in the E.R. Spends way too much time on the job, if you ask me. The man needs some diversions." Henry shot her a quick look over his shoulder.

At the speculative glint in his eyes, Marci smothered a sigh. First Edith had thrown out hints about the two of them getting together. Now Henry seemed tuned to the same channel.

Which was all the more reason to keep her distance, Marci reminded herself as Christopher glided to a stop beside them. There were way too many sparks flying already; the last thing they needed was any encouragement.

Still straddling the bike, Christopher took off his helmet and smiled at her.

The way her heart melted, you'd think she was some innocent, starry-eyed teen in the throes of her first crush, Marci thought in disgust. And she was none of the above.

"Hi, Marci."

"Hi." Her reply came out stiff. Almost unfriendly.

If he noticed, he didn't let on. But Henry pursed his lips and gave her an odd look before turning his attention to Christopher.

"Was the prescription ready?"

"Yes." Twisting around, Christopher snagged two grocery bags out of one of the wire baskets and handed them to the older man. "I think I got everything else on your list, too. And I threw in a couple of sugar doughnuts from The Flake."

"You didn't have to do that." Grinning, Henry reached for the bags. "But I'm glad you did."

"I thought you might be." Christopher winked and swung his leg over the bar on the bike. "There's a pair of garden gloves in there, too. For your new assistant. Gardening is hard on the hands." He turned to her. "How's the scratch?"

Was there anything this man *didn't* notice? Marci shoved her right hand deeper into her pocket to hide the long scratch down the back, a souvenir of yesterday's tussle with a rose bush.

She gave a slight shrug. "It's fine. I'll be happy to reimburse you for the gloves."

"No way," Henry protested. "If anyone's going to repay him, it's me. The cost of a pair of garden gloves is a small price to pay for all the free labor I'm getting."

"Forget it. It's no big deal." Christopher checked

his watch. "I need to grab a quick bite, then head to the hospital. See you later."

Without waiting for a response, he pushed his bike around the corner of his cottage.

"He's a good boy. Been almost like a son to me these past two years." Henry started toward the gate to the backyard.

"Let me take a bag, Henry." Marci gently tugged one of the plastic sacks out of his hand as they went through the gate, her curiosity piqued. "Have you only known him for two years?"

"Yep. That's when he moved to the island from Boston. Marjorie and I used to rent out the cottage to summer people, but when Christopher offered to sign a one-year lease, I grabbed it. It's a whole lot easier than having new people come and go all the time, and now I have income for the whole year, not just for the summer. It's worked out real fine. He renewed it for the second time last month. Can't imagine not having him around anymore. But I expect one of these days he'll go home."

Why? And why is he here in the first place?

Marci had to bite back the questions as they reached the back porch.

"Would you like me to bring this inside for you or hand it through the door, Henry?"

"Come on in." He pulled open the screen door and stepped aside to let her pass. "Don't mind the dust. I'm not much of a housekeeper."

Crossing the threshold, Marci walked through the small mud room and set the bag on the Formica counter in the kitchen. Though the room was dated, she liked its warmth. Yellow curtains added a bright spot of color, and a pine table for four was tucked into a windowed alcove that offered a view into the backyard and the sea beyond. Although she spotted some dust on the lower cabinets, the countertops were clutter free and the sink had been wiped clean. A dishrag was draped over the chrome faucet, and a neatly folded towel had been tucked into the handle of the oven.

A framed photo on the wall near the table caught her attention, and Marci moved closer to examine the scene of Henry's backyard. The gazebo was still in place, its weathered patina the color of driftwood. A slim older woman, a basket of cut flowers in hand, a pleasant smile softening her lips, stood at the entrance below a band of lattice.

"That's my Marjorie. I put that picture there so I can look at her while I eat. I never did like to eat alone."

At Henry's wistful tone, she shifted toward him. "Do you have any children, Henry?"

His expression grew melancholy. "A daughter. She lives in Boston. Doesn't get down this way much." He gave her a smile that seemed forced. "How about we get to work on that garden? With the clouds rolling in, I expect this will be a short day."

"Okay by me."

"Let me find those gloves Christopher bought. Mighty thoughtful of him. But that's the kind of man he is." He rummaged through the bag as he spoke. "Last winter I had a nasty bout of pneumonia. Was weak as a kitten for weeks. Christopher came over to see me twice a day and brought me food every night. Watched a lot of old movies with me, too, even though he had better things to do." He withdrew the gloves and handed them over.

Marci took them, fingering the soft leather. No cheap cloth gloves for Christopher Morgan. These were good quality. Expensive.

In other words, too nice for her.

She knew what J.C. would say about that sort of thinking. But even though her self-esteem was improving, her first reaction to such acts of kindness still tended to be that she wasn't worthy of such generosity.

For once, however, she didn't mistrust the gesture, as was her typical reaction with gifts from men. Christopher hadn't made her feel she was in his debt for the house call. Nor, she suspected, would he expect anything in return for this considerate gesture. His motives weren't suspect.

He seemed, as Henry had indicated, to simply be a good man.

The kind of man she'd always dreamed of finding.

But those dreams weren't likely to be fulfilled.

Because she didn't think she would ever feel worthy of someone like Christopher Morgan.

"So, where have you been keeping yourself? We've hardly seen you since we got back from our honeymoon." J.C. passed a bowl of mashed potatoes to Marci.

She took it and scooped a generous portion onto her plate, then handed it to Heather. "Do you know Henry Calhoun?"

Heather propped her elbows on the small oak table in the corner of The Devon Rose kitchen. "Isn't he the older gentleman in 'Sconset, J.C.? The one with the white picket fence that the church youth group painted last summer when my nephew was here?"

"Yeah. That's Henry. How do you know him?" J.C. asked Marci.

"He came to tea while you were gone, and we hit it off. He invited me to visit him, and while I was there we got to talking about how overgrown his garden was, and how his wife used to take such good care of it, and one thing led to another. Now I spend my mornings on the beach and my afternoons at Henry's playing in the dirt. He's a great guy. Eight-five years old. Taught English at the high school until he retired, and he still tutors. He's a trustee at the Lifesaving Museum, too."

"Wait a minute. Back up. You're doing yard work?" J.C. shot her a disapproving look. "This is supposed to be a vacation."

"Relax, J.C. It *is* a vacation. I don't have to get up at the crack of dawn to sling hash at Ronnie's. I don't have to stay up until two in the morning working on term papers or studying for tests. I'm living in a cottage that belongs in the pages of *House Beautiful*. My time is my own, and I'm loving every minute of it. But the truth is, I'm used to being busy. If all I did was sit around on the beach day after day, I'd go nuts."

J.C. studied her as he took a sip of water. "Is that how you got the scratch on your hand? Gardening?"

She shrugged. "Sometimes to uncover beauty you have to deal with a few thorns." A few seconds of silence ticked by as she examined the long, jagged abrasion. Then she summoned up a smile. "But this won't happen again. I have some garden gloves now."

"Did you get them at Bartlett's Farm? They have a great garden center."

Marci dug into her mashed potatoes, thinking fast. "No. Henry's neighbor offered me a pair. Heather, did you put some unusual seasoning in these? They're great."

"A touch of garlic salt."

"What neighbor?" J.C. persisted.

"What difference does it make?" Marci shot him a peeved look.

His eyes narrowed. "Why are you evading the question?"

"Why are you playing detective? You're supposed to be off duty now."

Heather looked from brother to sister. "Okay. Change of subject. J.C., show your sister the drawing from Nathan. You'll love it, Marci. We sent him a photo of The Devon Rose, and he did an incredible pen-and-ink sketch of it as a wedding present. It arrived while we were on our honeymoon. I'm going to frame it and hang it in the foyer."

For a few moments, J.C. continued to regard Marci. Then, with a sigh of capitulation, he rose to retrieve the rendering, handing it to his sister without a word.

Thank you, God, if you're listening, Marci said silently. The last thing she needed was to have her brother join the Nantucket matchmaking club. Now that he was married, she had a feeling he was going to be harping on her to start dating. He'd never understood why her social life was a big, fat zero. And she had no intention of enlightening him.

Taking the drawing, Marci set aside her fork and examined it. Both she and J.C. had been stunned last summer when they'd discovered their brother's incredible talent during their emotional reconciliation at the prison where he was serving time for armed robbery.

"He gets better and better, doesn't he?" Marci shook her head in wonder.

"Yes. I think he has a bright future ahead now that he's started down a new path."

"According to his last letter, it sounds like he's on track to finish his GED by the end of the summer." Marci handed the drawing back to J.C.

"That's the plan. He just needs to hang in for one more year."

"He wouldn't have such a hopeful future to look forward to without you," Marci said.

A flush crept across her brother's cheeks as he set the drawing aside. "God can take most of the credit for that."

Heather entwined her fingers with her husband's. "That's true. But without you, he wouldn't have found God, either. You did good with both of your siblings." She sent Marci a smile.

"I second that." Marci lifted her water glass in tribute to the one person in her life she had always been able to count on. Whose love for his siblings had never wavered, despite the trouble and heart-aches they'd given him.

There weren't too many guys like him around, Marci mused as she buttered a roll.

But she was beginning to think a certain 'Sconset doctor might qualify for membership in that exclusive club.

Chapter Five

Why wasn't Henry answering her knock?

Marci tapped her garden gloves against her palm. Usually he met her at the front door. But she was a few minutes late. Maybe he was waiting for her in the yard.

Circling the house, she paused to inhale the heady, old-fashioned scent of the pink roses clinging to the arbor that arched over the gate to the backyard. She'd spent a good part of one afternoon untwining the ivy and wild morning-glory vines from the hardy canes, and based on the profusion of buds she'd uncovered, the bush would be a show-stopper in another couple of weeks.

"Henry, are you back here?" Marci pushed through the gate, clicking it shut behind her.

No response.

Hmm. If he wasn't in the house or the yard, where was he?

A few seconds later, when she rounded the corner of the clapboard cottage and got a full view of the backyard, she got her answer.

The older man was lying on the ground, the bowl of the concrete birdbath upside down on his chest. And he wasn't moving.

She froze, her heart slamming against her rib cage. Pulse pounding, she raced across the lawn and dropped down beside him. Reached for his hand. It was cold.

"Henry? Henry, can you hear me?"

At her frantic question, his eyelids fluttered open. For a moment he seemed disoriented. Then he blinked and slowly focused. "Hey, Marci. Got myself…into a real pickle… didn't I?"

The words were gasped rather than spoken. And etched with pain.

But at least he was conscious. That was a good sign. She hoped.

"Don't move, Henry."

"Can't. That's why…I'm here."

She tried to stay calm. Think logically. Okay, the bowl of the birdbath was resting on the ground on Henry's left side. That would give her some leverage to push it off without putting any more pressure on his chest.

Moving to his right side, Marci knelt and grasped the elevated edge of the bowl. "I'm going to lift this off of you, Henry. Hang on."

She took a deep breath. Tightened her grip. Raised the oversized concrete basin inch by inch, her muscles straining. The thing weighed a ton.

When it was standing on end on Henry's left side, she rose and stepped over him, keeping a firm grip on the concrete edge. Then she lowered the bowl to the ground.

"That's a relief. Thank you."

Henry started to move, but Marci pressed him back with a hand on his shoulder as she knelt beside him. He was way too pale, and his skin still felt cold. And clammy. "We need to get you checked out by the EMTs. Does anything hurt?"

"My left side is kind of sore. Might have cracked a rib." He blinked up at her again. "You look a little fuzzy, too."

She fumbled in her purse for her cell phone, her fingers shaking so badly it took her two tries to punch in 911. As she waited for the call to go through, she rested one hand on Henry's shoulder and did her best to sound calm. "Just stay still, Henry. Help will be here soon."

While answering the dispatcher's questions, Marci kept an eye on the older man. His eyelids had drifted closed again, and she took his hand, pressing her thumb to his wrist.

"Ticker's still working, if that's what you're checking," he told her wryly.

Despite the gravity of the situation, her lips twitched at his humor.

Ending the call, Marci shoved the phone back into her purse. "The ambulance is on the way."

"Last time an ambulance came here was when Marjorie had her heart attack. She never came home."

Marci's throat constricted at his melancholy tone. "This isn't a heart attack. You'll be back. We're not done with the garden yet."

A whisper of a smile touched his lips, and he gave her hand a gentle squeeze. "You're a good girl, Marci."

His voice was weakening, and another wave of panic washed over her. "How long ago did you fall, Henry?"

"I came out about noon. Thought I'd get the birdbath out of our way, since we were going to work in that section today. Guess I'm not as strong as I thought I was. Used to be able to lift stuff like that with no problem. But I twisted my ankle when I turned and lost my balance. Fell back with the bowl on top of me. Not my most graceful moment."

She checked her watch. He'd been lying out here fifteen minutes before she arrived. Not good.

The faint wail of a siren pierced the air. Although it was a seven-mile trip from the main town, she figured the ambulance would make good time on Milestone Road.

But it couldn't get here fast enough to suit her.

"Sorry for all this trouble, Marci."

Henry's apology tugged at her heart. "It's no trouble, Henry. I just want you to get back on your feet fast so we can finish this garden before I leave."

He squinted up at her, as if trying to focus, and his grip loosened. "Might not happen, Marci."

"Of course it will."

Another smile whispered at his lips. "I like your spirit. You'd be good for Christopher, you know. That boy needs a woman like you."

He was starting to drift, and Marci didn't respond. The *last* thing Christopher needed was a woman like her—for reasons she didn't want to get into with Henry. Why tarnish her relationship with the older man by introducing bad stuff from her past?

The minutes passed in slow motion, but at last she caught a glimpse of flashing lights as the wailing ambulance came down the tiny byway in front of the cottage. Only when the EMTs pushed through the back gate did she relinquish her grip on Henry's hand.

She stepped aside as they went to work, answering their questions while they started an IV and took Henry's vitals. Most of the terminology they bantered back and forth was Greek to her, but she gleaned enough to determine that his blood pressure was low and that they were concerned about the pain on his left side.

When the EMTs were ready to transport him, Henry turned her way. "Would you call Christopher, Marci?"

"Sure. And I'll follow you to the hospital, too."

He lifted a hand in acknowledgment, then closed his eyes again.

As the technicians loaded Henry into the ambulance, Marci slid into her car, following the ambulance when it began to pull away from Henry's cottage.

By the time she finally got a live operator on the phone for directory assistance and was put through to Christopher's office, she was back on Milestone Road, headed for the main town.

"Family Medical offices. How may I help you?"

"I'm trying to reach Dr. Morgan. Is he in?"

"Yes. He's with a patient. May I have him return your call later this afternoon?"

"I'd appreciate it if you'd give him a message as soon as possible. This is Marci Clay. Would you let him know that Henry Calhoun has had an accident? He's en route to the E.R. now. Let me give you my cell number." Marci recited it.

"I'll catch him between patients."

With a murmured thank-you, Marci set the phone in her lap.

Less than five minutes later, it rang. "Christopher?"

"Yes. What happened?"

She could hear the worry in his clipped question. Keeping her narrative as brief as possible, she gave him the highlights.

"His color wasn't good, and he said his left side hurt. Do you think he might have broken some ribs?" she finished.

"It's possible. I'll call the E.R. and let them know I want to be kept informed. Where are you?"

"Following the ambulance."

"I'll get to the hospital as soon as I can, but I've got a full patient load this afternoon. I'll call you if I hear any news."

"Thanks."

There was a brief pause.

"How are *you* doing?"

His quiet, caring question took her off guard. "I'm not the one who fell."

"Accidents are traumatic on everyone."

At the warmth in his voice, Marci blinked away the tears that sprang to her eyes. "It was scary. And I didn't like feeling helpless." A tremor ran through her words, and she clamped her lips together. She was *not* going to get emotional, even if she was touched by his unexpected concern. It wasn't in keeping with the strong, independent image she cultivated.

Adopting a bravado she didn't feel, she hardened her tone. "But, hey, I'm a tough chick. You don't have to worry about me."

In the few beats of silence that followed, Marci got the distinct impression she hadn't fooled Christopher.

"Okay. Hang in there. We'll get him through this. I'll be in touch."

The line went dead, and Marci dropped the phone back into her lap, mulling over his last comment. *We'll* get him through this, he'd said. Like they'd work together to cope with whatever lay ahead. As partners.

That *we* had a nice sound to it, she reflected wistfully.

Christopher swung into the hospital parking lot and propped his bike against the back wall of the E.R. He'd hated to leave in the middle of office hours. It would put him way behind and aggravate waiting patients. But the news he'd received ten minutes ago had warranted a quick trip to the hospital.

Pushing through the staff entrance, he saw the senior doctor on duty getting ready to enter an examining room.

"Jack."

The fiftyish man with salt-and-pepper hair turned at the summons, waiting as Christopher joined him.

"Where's Henry?"

"Room three. He's being prepped."

"I'll make a quick stop there first. I also want to take a look at the CT scan. Is David here?" David Clark was a good surgeon, and Christopher was comfortable putting Henry in his hands.

"He's on his way."

With a curt nod, Christopher strode toward room three. Two nurses were with Henry, but they edged aside to allow him to move in close.

Christopher's stomach knotted as he assessed Henry. In the two years he'd known him, the man had become like a second grandfather. Other than the bout with pneumonia, he'd always been healthy.

But he didn't look healthy now. His color was bad, and deep crevices lined his face. Under the sheet, his thin frame seemed barely there.

As if sensing his presence, Henry opened his eyes.

"Hey, Christopher."

"Hello, Henry. I hear you had a fall."

"Yep. They gave me the bad news."

"You okay with the plan?"

"Do I have a choice?"

"Yes. But this is what I'd recommend."

"That's what they told me. So I said go ahead." He reached out a hand, and Christopher took his gnarled fingers. "Thanks for coming, Christopher. Sorry for the bother."

His throat tightened. "It's no bother, Henry. Marci's here, too."

"I know. They told me. Go find her and tell her to go home. No sense wasting time at a hospital unless you get hauled here like I did."

"I'll see what I can do. I called your daughter, too."

Henry made a face. "I bet she threw a hissy fit."

"Not quite." But close, Christopher admitted. He'd had to listen to a rant about stubborn old men who refused to listen to reason. More than once during the tirade he'd had to bite his tongue. "She's coming down tomorrow."

Henry sighed. "Better batten down the hatches." Pulling his hand free of Christopher's, he waved him toward the door. "Go see that little lady in the waiting room. And tell her not to worry about me. If it's my time, it's my time. I'm ready. Besides, there's no sense fretting over spilled milk. Or foolish old men."

"It isn't your time. Not if we have anything to say about it. And we'll talk about the foolish part later." He took Henry's hand again and gave it an encouraging squeeze. "God be with you, my friend."

Exiting the examining room, he commandeered one of the E.R. computers and pulled up Henry's CT scan.

As he studied it, the senior doctor joined him. "What do you think?"

"Same thing you do. Grade two, borderline three." Christopher pointed to the abdominal cavity. "We may need to transfuse."

"Agreed. We're keeping a close eye on blood count and pressure."

With a nod, Christopher stood. "A friend of Henry's is in the waiting room. I'll brief her before I head back to the office. Call me with any updates, okay?"

"Sure."

Striding through the E.R. intake area, Christopher stepped into the large waiting room. A number of people were lounging in the chairs, reading magazines or newspapers, and they all looked up when he entered. He didn't see Marci.

Only after he moved farther into the irregularly shaped room did he spot her. She was staring out a window in the far corner, arms crossed tight over her chest, posture rigid, her distress almost palpable. She might try to present a tough front to the world, but he'd caught enough candid glimpses of her to know that beneath that veneer she had a tender, caring heart. This unguarded moment confirmed his conclusion.

As he closed the distance between them, the movement caught her attention, and she turned. Her complexion went a shade paler, and her eyes widened in alarm.

"What are you doing here? Is Henry..." Her voice choked.

"No." He took her arm and eased her into a chair, fighting off a sudden urge to pull her into a hug that was part comfort and part something much more. Clearing his throat, he retrieved his hand. "I came over between patients."

"Why?" She searched his eyes. "It's more than a cracked rib, isn't it?"

"Yes. His ribs are fine. But he has a lacerated spleen. And some internal bleeding."

She squeezed her eyes shut, took a deep breath, then opened them.

"I had a feeling it was bad. What happens now?"

"If Henry was younger, we might take a conservative approach and see if the spleen would heal on its own. But that treatment option hasn't been very successful in patients over fifty-five. So we're going to remove it."

"What's the downside of that?"

"Short-term, the typical risks of any surgery. Long-term, greater susceptibility to infections."

Marci frowned and clasped her hands in her lap. "How long will the surgery take?"

"Two or three hours. Henry said I should tell you to go home."

"Forget it."

"I had a feeling you'd say that."

"How long will he be in here?"

"If all goes well, four or five days."

"Then what?"

"I'm not sure. Recovery can take months. And he'll need a fair amount of help initially."

She turned to look out the window, giving him a view of her pensive profile. "When we were waiting for the ambulance, he told me his wife never came home after she was taken to the hospital." She looked back at him, her expression troubled. "I sensed he might be thinking that will be true for him, too."

"I got the same impression. But I'm going to do everything I can to make certain that doesn't happen. Henry's very active and healthy for his age. Other than arthritis, not much slows him down. There's no reason he can't recover from this—unless he gives up."

"He's not the type to do that."

"That might change if his independence is compromised. Or if he has to leave his cottage. I've seen it happen."

Marci's perceptive gaze softened as she studied him. "You're not talking about your experience with patients, are you?"

The woman across from him might be fair-haired and beautiful, but no way did she fit the dumb-blonde stereotype. Her insights were way too sharp. And her well of compassion—and empathy—seemed to run deep. He had a feeling she'd excel at social work.

"No. I saw it happen with my grandfather." He was tempted to tell her more, but a quick check of his watch confirmed there was no time for a prolonged discussion. "I have a waiting room full of patients to see, but I'll be back as soon as I can. In the meantime, I'll be in touch with the hospital, and I'll give you a call if there's any news. You might want to run home for a while, Marci. Henry's right.

There's nothing you can do here while he's in surgery."

She shrugged and stared at the toe of her sports shoe. "Leaving doesn't feel right. It would be sad to be in surgery and think no one cared enough to hang around." Raising her chin, she met his gaze. "Would you tell him I'm staying?"

Christopher's throat tightened, and he touched her hand for a brief second before he stood. "Yes. I'll run back and talk to him before I leave."

"Thanks." She slumped against the wall, refolding her arms across her chest. Looking once more as if she could use a hug.

For a fleeting instant, Christopher was again tempted to follow his instincts and wrap her in his arms. To hold her close and assure her Henry would be fine.

But Marci had done nothing to encourage that kind of gesture.

And he didn't know what the future held for Henry.

Chapter Six

After her stomach rumbled for the third time, Marci rose and started pacing, hoping moving would quiet its complaints. Or mask the noise, if nothing else.

Three hours had passed since Christopher had left her in the waiting room, and the cast of characters around her had turned over at least twice. In all that time, there'd been no word about Henry.

Nada.

Zip.

Zilch.

Had everyone forgotten she was here? Including Christopher?

Deciding to throw herself on the mercy of the woman at the E.R. intake desk, she turned that direction—just as Christopher pushed through the door.

Her pulse leapt, and she met him halfway as he wove through the room. "Well?"

"He's out of surgery. Everything went well, and he didn't need a transfusion. He'll be in recovery for a while, then moved to a regular room later tonight."

The tension in her shoulders eased. "Can I see him?"

"Not yet. He won't be coherent for an hour or two."

Her stomach rumbled again, and Marci's cheeks grew warm. "Sorry. Must be the stress."

"Or hunger. Did you eat lunch?"

"I had some yogurt. I wasn't that hungry."

"Sounds like you are now. Why don't we grab a quick bite? By the time we're through, you should be able to see him for a few minutes."

Before she could process the unexpected invitation, her phone began to vibrate. *Saved by the bell,* she thought, grateful for the interruption as she retrieved it from her pocket.

"Excuse me for a minute." She put the phone to her ear. "Hello."

"Marci? Are you okay? We got worried when you didn't return the car."

"Hi, J.C. Yeah, I'm fine. Henry had an accident, and I've been at the E.R. all afternoon."

"Is he okay?"

She gave him a quick rundown. "If you don't need the car tonight I'd like to hang around a while," she finished.

"No. We're planning a quiet evening at home. You want us to bring you over some dinner?"

She glanced at Christopher, who'd taken a discreet step back. "I, uh, already have other plans."

"With who? I didn't think you knew anyone here other than me and Heather and Edith and Chester." A few beats of silence ticked by. "Except Henry's neighbor. The doctor. Otherwise known as 'the glove man,' maybe?"

No wonder her brother was such a good detective, Marci thought in annoyance. "No comment."

"That tells me all I need to know. And good for you. It's about time you went out on a date."

"It's not a…" She shot Christopher a quick look. He raised an eyebrow and she huffed out a breath. "Good bye, J.C." She said the words very deliberately and punched the end button with more force than necessary.

"Your brother?" Christopher took a step closer.

"Yeah." She dropped the phone into her purse. "How did you know?"

"I recognize the initials. We attend the same church, and I've run into him a few times in the E.R. when he was on duty. Seems like a nice guy."

"He is. Also nosy."

Christopher flashed her a smile. "I know what it's like to have a big brother always looking over your shoulder. And I expect it's worse for a younger sister. So how about some food? Downyflake is only a five-minute walk. I'll have my pager with me, if anything comes up with Henry."

The local hangout was a family place, with bright lights and no hint of romance. It was perfect.

And she was starving.

"Sounds good."

"Let's go, then. But watch your step. They're replacing some of the slabs in the sidewalk."

He took her arm as they exited the E.R. It was an impersonal, polite gesture indicative of breeding and good manners—and nothing more, Marci knew. Just as she knew the warm spot on her arm where his fingers connected with her skin would soon grow cold again.

But as they headed down the sidewalk, his protective hand guiding her around the rough patches, she let herself pretend for just a few minutes that his touch meant far more.

Fifteen minutes later, seated on opposite sides of a booth, they dived into hearty bowls of quahog chowder.

"This is great." Marci added a few more oyster crackers to her bowl and stirred them in.

"It's hard to go wrong with the local specialty."

"I've only had it one other time since I've been here."

"The night I saw you in the restaurant."

She gave him a startled look, and heat crept up Christopher's neck. He hadn't intended to bring up their first encounter. The comment had just popped out. Perhaps because it had been on his mind for the past few days. As had her distress that evening—and the comparison to Denise it had evoked.

The more he saw of Marci, though, the less he believed that link was valid. Denise had been clingy and needy. Marci struck him as strong and independent. Unlike Denise, whose mood swings were volatile, Marci's personality was generally on an even keel. While tears had been a daily fact of life for Denise, Christopher suspected they were a rare occurrence for Marci.

Yet she'd been crying that night in the restaurant. Meaning if his hypothesis was accurate, something big had rattled her. But what?

"I'm surprised you noticed what I was eating. I got the distinct impression your attention was elsewhere."

At Marci's saucy comeback and smile, the flush on his neck rose higher. "Guilty as charged. A lapse for which I've already apologized. But the truth is, while I've come to admire a lot of other things about you since that night, you *do* have great legs."

Now it was her turn to blush. But he also saw a flash of that poignant sadness in her eyes. "Unfortunately, my physical assets are often the only thing people notice."

He stirred his chowder. "I noticed more than that."

"Right. My soup."

"No. I also noticed you were crying. In all honesty, that's the *first* thing I noticed."

She bit her lower lip between her teeth. "I don't usually cry in public."

He'd half expected her to deny it. The fact that she hadn't, felt somehow like a victory—though he wasn't certain why.

"I already came to that conclusion. Which makes me wonder what happened to bring on tears."

She shrugged and stared down into her chowder. "J.C. and Heather got married that afternoon. I guess I was just caught up in the emotions of the day."

Her refusal to meet his gaze told him she was hiding something. That there was a lot more to the story—and she wasn't willing to share it.

As if to confirm his conclusion, she spooned some chowder into her mouth and changed the subject.

"Tell me about the grandfather you mentioned earlier."

No sense pushing tonight, he decided. But his curiosity was more piqued than ever. Maybe if he opened up a bit about his background, she would reciprocate.

"Pop was a great guy. My dad's father died when I was very young, so my mom's father was the only grandfather I ever knew. We had some fabulous times." A smile of reminiscence tugged at his lips. "He lived in a small town about an hour north of Boston, and he used to take my brother and I sailing every Saturday in the summer. He'd built the boat himself years before. It wasn't big or fancy, but it gave us priceless memories. And I learned a lot from him. About self-reliance and initiative and courage. Not a day goes by that I don't miss him."

Emotion clogged his throat, and Christopher coughed, working to regain his composure.

As if sensing his need to regroup, Marci ate in silence for a minute before broaching another question. "What happened to him?"

He wiped his lips with a paper napkin and balled it into his fist. "He had a stroke six years ago. Pop made some bad investments in later years and didn't have much money. My parents and my brother and I all offered him financial help, but he refused. He said he didn't want to be a burden to anyone. Without telling us, he sold his house. Then he moved into an assisted-living facility."

Christopher jabbed at one of the crackers in his chowder with his spoon until it disappeared beneath the surface. "He only lasted six months. He just withered away and died."

"That's why you help Henry so much, isn't it?"

At Marci's soft question, he looked up to find her watching him with a tender expression that made him want to learn more about her. A lot more. He started to reach for her hand as he responded. "That's part of…"

"Here you go, sweetie." The middle-aged waitress bustled up to the table and slid a plate in front of Marci. "And the special for you, Doc." She set the second plate in front of Christopher as he retracted his hand. "Enjoy."

Rather than dive into her food, Marci tucked her hands in her lap. Telling him she'd noticed his impulsive gesture and didn't welcome it. Picking up his fork, he stifled a surprisingly strong surge of disappointment and tried to shift gears. "My experience with my grandfather did give me a lot of empathy for the needs of the elderly. I'd hate to see Henry end up in the same situation as Pop."

"I thought you said he should be able to go home once he recovers." She eased a hand over to the ketchup bottle and squirted some on her plate. The slight tremble in her fingers was telling.

"That's true. But his daughter will fight it. She's been after him for the past few years to either move into a retirement home on the island or go live with her in Boston. This will give her an excuse to renew that crusade. And in light of his weakened condition, she may wear him down this time. But his whole life and all his memories are connected to that cottage. Take him away from that, and he'll be finished."

"Why is she pushing so hard?"

Christopher speared some broccoli as he debated

how to answer. "I've only met her once, but my impression wasn't too favorable. I think she'd like to sell the cottages. Property on Nantucket is outrageously expensive, and Henry's two houses are worth a lot."

"Does she need money?"

A mirthless smile twisted his lips. "Depends on how you define 'need.' She married into wealth, lives in a very nice home in one of Boston's most desirable neighborhoods, travels quite a bit, wears designer clothes. But I suppose there's always another cruise to take or diamond ring to buy."

Marci frowned. "She doesn't sound like a very nice person."

"Suffice it to say, she and Henry are night and day."

"There has to be something we can do to override whatever pressure she puts on him. I'm sure we can find a way to help him stay in his house."

Her determined tone reinforced Christopher's impression that Marci Clay could be a force to be reckoned with once she set her mind to a task. "Sounds like Henry has another champion."

She shrugged. "I like him. And I admire independence."

"So do I." He pinned her with an intent look and a soft flush stole across her cheeks. "Maybe between the two of us we can come up with a plan. But first we need to help him get through the next few days." He took a bite of his flounder. "Let's finish up and go pay the patient a visit."

Twenty minutes later, as they approached the door to the recovery room, Christopher paused and turned to Marci. "Have you been in hospitals much?"

"No."

"Don't let all the equipment disturb you. We'll be keeping a close watch on him for the first day or two."

"Okay."

He pushed the door open and moved aside to let her enter.

Marci was glad Christopher had prepared her. Henry's bed was surrounded by all sorts of machines emitting odd noises, their digital screens displaying a dizzying array of data.

When she faltered, she felt a comforting hand in the small of her back.

"You okay?"

He spoke close to her ear, his breath warm on her cheek. Good thing she wasn't hooked up to that heart monitor, Marci reflected, eying the steady blip indicating Henry's pulse. Her reading would be off the charts.

She gave a brief nod.

With his hand urging her forward, she moved beside Henry's bed.

"Everything okay?" Christopher asked the nurse on the other side of the room.

"He's doing great."

Henry's eyelids flickered open, and he squinted up at them.

"That you, Christopher?"

"It's me, Henry. Marci's with me."

She moved into Henry's line of sight. Closer to Christopher. She assumed he'd shift back slightly, but he didn't. Instead, he angled his body until her shoulder was brushing his chest. Which did nothing to steady her pulse.

"Hi, Henry." Her words wavered.

"You should have gone home, Marci."

"I wanted to stay." She leaned closer and took his hand. "How do you feel? Are you in any pain?"

"Not feeling much of anything at the moment. They must have given me some mighty powerful drugs. What time is it?"

Christopher checked his watch. "Eight-thirty."

"Go home. Don't put in any overtime on my account. You, too, Marci. The two of you have better things to do than sit around an old man's bedside. And if you don't, you ought to."

A deep chuckle rumbled behind Marci, and she

felt the pleasant weight of Christopher's hand on her shoulder. "I think we're being kicked out, Marci."

Every instinct in her body told her to lean back. To rest against his broad chest. To let his solid strength support her.

But she wasn't a leaner. Never had been. It was safer to stand on your own two feet. To count on no one but yourself.

Bending to press a light kiss to Henry's forehead, she used that as an excuse to disengage from Christopher's hand. "We get the message, Henry. I'll be back tomorrow."

He gripped her hand and gave it a squeeze. "Thanks a lot for hanging around today. I didn't expect it, but it sure made me feel good." He angled his head to peer around her. "Why don't you take this pretty little lady out for a bite to eat, Christopher?"

"I already did."

Henry's eyebrows rose and he gave his tenant a pleased smile. "Did you, now? Well, maybe there's hope for you yet."

Marci closed her eyes. Henry was as bad as Edith when it came to matchmaking. Dipping her head, she rummaged around in her purse, taking far longer than necessary to find her keys. When at last she pulled them out, she pasted on a bright smile. "I guess I'll head out."

"I'll walk you to your car."

She shook her head, playing with her keys instead of looking at Christopher. "That's not necessary."

"Always let a gentleman be a gentleman, Marci." This from Henry, who seemed to be enjoying the little drama playing out at his bedside.

"I'm used to taking care of myself."

"Good manners trump independence," Christopher chimed in.

She turned to him. "Who says?"

He stuck one hand in the pocket of his slacks and gave her a half smile. "Letitia Baldridge."

Marci narrowed her eyes. Who was Letitia Baldridge? Some etiquette guru, maybe?

"He's right, Marci," Henry chimed in.

She was outvoted, and she knew it. Making an issue of it would only raise suspicions.

"Okay. Fine." Settling the strap of her purse higher on her shoulder, she edged past him toward the door. "'Bye, Henry."

"See you later, Marci."

She waited in the hall as the two men had a brief exchange in voices too low to decipher. When Christopher joined her he was smiling.

"He's in good spirits tonight." Then his smile faded. "I hope it lasts once his daughter arrives. Where are you parked?"

"Not far from the E.R. entrance."

He fell into step beside her, and as they exited the building into the deepening twilight, she surveyed the dark clouds overhead. "Looks like we're in for a storm."

"Yeah. I hope I make it home before it hits."

Her step faltered. "Did you ride your bike to work today?"

"Yes." He gestured toward the sky. "This is one of the downsides. Weather on an island can be changeable. But it won't be the first time I've battled the elements on my bike. Is that your car?" He nodded to a late-model compact in the mostly deserted lot.

"Yeah. Look, I can't let you ride your bike all the way home in threatening weather. Besides, it's getting dark. And you've had a long day."

"You've had a long day, too. And 'Sconset isn't exactly on your route home."

"At this point, adding another twenty or thirty minutes to my day isn't going to make a whole lot of difference."

He flashed her a brief grin and turned his hands up in capitulation. "You don't have to strong-arm me. I can drive in tomorrow and pick up my bike before I go to the office. Give me a minute to stow it inside."

As she watched him stride toward the back of the building, Marci leaned against the car and scanned the sky once more. Had it remained clear, she would have let Christopher bike home.

But she didn't mind the extra trip to 'Sconset.

Or the extra time with Christopher.

Even if that was a very dangerous sign.

"We may beat the storm after all." Christopher turned to study Marci as she focused on the road ahead in the dwindling light. She'd said little for the past two miles, and his attempts to draw her out had produced brief replies. He was picking up some tension that he sensed was unrelated to her stressful day.

"Maybe."

"Are you tired?"

She shot him a quick glance. "Why?"

"You're not very talkative."

Twin furrows appeared on her brow. "Sorry. I've been thinking about Henry. He's lucky to have someone like you who cares so much about him."

"He's a great guy. I liked him the minute we met. You must feel the same way, or you wouldn't be hanging around his place every day."

"I never knew my grandparents. He already sort of feels like one."

"Did they die when you were young?"

"My mom's father died before I was born, and her mother died when I was two. I have no memory of my father's parents. And no good ones of my father."

At the underlying bitterness in her final, tacked-on comment, he frowned. "Is your father still living?"

"I don't know. He deserted our family when I was eleven."

He took a deep breath and gentled his voice. "I'm sorry, Marci."

She gave a stiff shrug. "Don't be. He drank too much and had a mean streak a mile wide. No one missed him. It was hard on my mom financially, though. She got a second job to make ends meet—until she was killed two years later in a hit-and-run accident. J.C. ended up raising us while he was practically a kid himself. He did his best, but we lived a bare-bones life in a rough neighborhood for a lot of years."

Christopher stared at her profile, noting the firm set of her chin. With all those tough breaks, it was no wonder she'd developed a thick skin. "Is your background the reason you went into social work?"

"Yeah. I know what it's like to live in that kind of environment. Trite as it may sound, I'm hoping I can make a difference in someone's life."

"You mentioned *us* earlier. Do you have other siblings besides J.C.?"

"A brother. Two years older than me." She flexed her fingers on the steering wheel. "So, tell me about you, Christopher. Are your parents living? And any siblings besides the brother you mentioned?"

The subject of her background was closed for the night, he realized. But that was okay. He'd learned more than he'd expected.

"Yes. They live in Boston. My brother and his wife and two kids live there, too."

"Is that where you lived before you came here?"

"Yes."

"Henry said you've been on the island two years. What brought you here?"

That was *not* a subject he wanted to discuss tonight.

Cracking his window, he took a breath of fresh air and chose his words with care. "We always vacationed here for three weeks in the summer when I was a kid. It's a very special place."

"But didn't you already have an established practice in Boston?"

"Yes."

"Are you going back at some point?"

"I'm not sure." Time to change the subject again. "What are your plans for tomorrow?"

She gave him a bemused look. "In other words, butt out?"

He sighed. "It's a long story, Marci. We've had enough drama for one day."

To his relief, she accepted his explanation as she drove down the quiet streets of 'Sconset and turned onto the byway Henry called home. Perhaps because she, too, had secrets she didn't want to share?

Pulling up in front of his cottage, she set the brake. "I want to run around the back and get my garden gloves before it rains. I dropped them in the midst of all the excitement."

"I'll go with you. If the birdbath is on the lawn, I can roll it aside. Henry won't be happy if he finds a dead spot in his grass."

He followed her around back, passing under the fragrant-smelling roses on the arbor. Marci picked up her gloves, then walked over to where Christopher was surveying the bowl of the birdbath.

"I can't believe he tried to lift this himself." Christopher shook his head. "I've warned him over and over not to take any chances. But he still thinks of himself as thirty."

"That's probably what keeps him young."

"True. But prudence has to come into play, too."

Dropping to a crouch, he grasped the edge of the bowl and heaved it upright. Somewhere along the way, he'd turned up the sleeves of his dress shirt, and Marci found herself admiring the way the muscles in his forearms bunched as he lifted the bowl until it was balanced on edge like a wheel. She watched as he rolled it to the open area that had once housed the gazebo. After lowering it to the ground, he returned to her side.

"You never answered my question."

She tried to focus, but she was still thinking about those muscular arms. For someone in a mostly sedentary occupation, he was in great shape. "Which one?"

"About your plans for tomorrow."

"Oh. Right. I'll, uh, probably go to see Henry in the morning, then come out here and work for a while. I'll stop by and visit him again on my way home."

"What happened to your beach time?"

She wrinkled her nose. "A little bit goes a long way. I don't think I have the constitution for sitting around doing nothing."

"Henry told me you put yourself through school working as a waitress." He shoved his hands into his pockets. "It doesn't sound like you've had much down time in your life."

It was too dim to read his expression, but she had no trouble interpreting his empathetic tone. No one except J.C. had ever cared how hard she'd worked to reach her goals.

Folding her arms across her chest, she hid her emotional reaction by turning the tables. "According to Henry, you don't, either."

A gust of wind whipped past, blowing her hair in her eyes, and Marci reached up to brush it aside.

One of the gloves slipped from her fingers, and she bent to retrieve it.

So did Christopher.

Their hands brushed, and her gaze flew to his as a distant flash of lightning illuminated the sky. Staring into those intense blue eyes mere inches away, she couldn't move. Couldn't breathe. Couldn't think.

All she could do was feel.

And the power of her feelings scared her.

Never in all of her thirty-one years had she experienced an attraction like this. Not even with the man who'd broken her heart.

There was no question in her mind that Christopher felt the pull as strongly as she did. She could feel it in the sudden tension in the air. And if she *had* had any doubts, they vanished when he lifted a hand and gently brushed her wind-tossed hair back from her face, his fingertips leaving a trail of warmth in their wake as he leaned toward her.

Marci didn't know what might have happened next, because all at once the heavens opened up.

As the sudden deluge jolted her to her senses, she dropped the other glove, sprang to her feet and stumbled back a few steps. "I'll see you around."

Then she took off at a run for her car.

Five minutes and several miles later, her pulse

finally began to return to normal. But that didn't change the facts.

Christopher had almost kissed her.

Marci wanted to believe she'd have found the strength to back away. To be smart. To set a clear limit on a relationship that had no future.

But as the rain hammered against the car, she knew that if not for the sudden shower, she might have tossed logic aside and given in to the yearning in her heart.

Though she wasn't much of a believer, she decided to consider the shower a warning from God. A divine caution sign.

Because no matter how appealing she found Christopher Morgan, he deserved better than the likes of her.

Chapter Seven

"Well, look who's here again! Rather see me than eat lunch, I guess."

At Henry's perky greeting, Christopher grinned. The older man's color had improved since early that morning, and his eyes were brighter.

Fitting his stethoscope into his ears, he gestured toward the large bouquet of flowers on the nightstand. "Nice."

"Marci brought them."

Why was he not surprised? "When did she visit?"

"Came about fifteen minutes ago. She just ran out to refill my water pitcher."

Which meant she was still here.

Not good. After that charged moment in Henry's backyard, he'd hoped to avoid her today. And in light of her quick exit last night, he suspected the feeling was mutual. They needed to give the interest flaring to life between them a chance to dissipate before another encounter. Maybe he could escape before...

"Okay, Henry, you're all..."

Too late.

As Marci's unfinished sentence hung in the air, Christopher removed the stethoscope from his ears and forced himself to turn toward the door.

She was hovering on the threshold as if debating whether to bolt. Her gaze met his for a fraction of a second before it darted to Henry.

"Come on in, Marci. You can set that next to the flowers you brought."

She shot Christopher another quick glance and edged around the far side of the bed to deposit the pitcher.

Henry looked back and forth between the two of them. "Something going on here I don't know about?"

Christopher forced his lips into the semblance of a smile. "Of course not. Are you heading out to work on the garden today?" He strove for a casual tone as he directed the question to Marci.

"Yes. That's my next stop. And I'm running way behind." She picked up her purse. "I'll come by on my way home, Henry. And you have my cell number if you want to call for any reason. I'll keep the phone in my pocket."

"I'll be fine. This is a first-class operation. Thanks again for the flowers."

Marci gave him a brief grin. "Actually, you can thank my sister-in-law. I raided her garden and—"

"I'm looking for Henry Calhoun's room. Would someone please direct me?"

As the imperious voice echoed down the hall outside Henry's room, the older man closed his eyes and gave a slight groan. "Let the games begin."

Marci shot Christopher a questioning look, and he mouthed the answer.

His daughter.

She rolled her eyes.

Five seconds later, Patricia Lawrence made her entrance. She hadn't changed much in the past year, Christopher noted, giving her a quick sweep. Same short hairstyle. Same flawless makeup. Same chic, designer clothes that couldn't hide the extra twenty pounds on her fifty-year-old frame. She did look a bit younger than he remembered. Botox, no doubt.

Patricia's eyes narrowed when she saw Marci, though she ignored the younger woman.

"Is he sleeping?" She scrutinized her father as she asked the question.

Henry opened his eyes. "No, Patricia, he isn't sleeping."

Her lips thinned. "Hello, Dad. Dr. Morgan." She acknowledged him with a nod, then raised an eyebrow at Marci. "I don't believe we've met."

"This is Marci Clay," Henry told her. "Marci, my daughter, Patricia Lawrence."

Marci moved toward the end of the bed and extended her hand. "Nice to meet you."

The woman took Marci's hand. Briefly. Said nothing. Then she turned back to him.

"I'd like to hear about his condition, Doctor." She shot Marci a pointed look. "Is there somewhere private we could speak?"

A flush suffused Marci's face, but before she could respond, Henry chimed in.

"You can speak right here. I have a right to hear whatever is said. And if it wasn't for Marci, I might still be lying in the yard with that birdbath on top of me. Plus, she spent most of yesterday keeping a vigil in the E.R. She can hear anything Christopher has to say."

Bright spots of color appeared on Patricia's cheeks. "Fine. Doctor?"

As Christopher briefed her on her father's condition, he kept tabs on Marci in his peripheral vision. She'd backed as close to the wall as she could get in the confined space and was fidgeting with her purse. He found himself struggling to maintain a cool, professional tone when what he really wanted to do was tell Patricia off for making Marci feel uncomfortable. And unwelcome.

"So, when will he be released?" Patricia asked as he finished.

"If he continues to do well, in four or five days."

"How much help will he need after that?"

"Quite a bit for the first week to ten days."

"Well, we'll have to arrange for assisted living." She tucked her Coach purse under her arm. "I certainly can't stay that long. I have commitments in Boston. I'm chairing a fund-raiser for the zoo a week from tomorrow, and the preceding few days will be crazy."

"I'm not going into assisted living, Patricia."

At Henry's pronouncement, her lips turned down in disapproval. "Don't be stubborn, Dad. This is the best solution."

"For you, maybe."

She glared at him. "You make it sound as if I'm selfish."

"If the shoe fits…"

"Well." She sniffed. "That's a fine thing to say after I came all the way down here from Boston. Do you realize I had to be at the airport at seven this morning? And I cancelled out of a dinner party tonight that's very important to Jonathan's career so I could be with you. Plus, I had to rearrange my entire schedule for Monday to accommodate this trip. My hairdresser was *not* pleased. How in the world can you call that selfish?"

Henry closed his eyes, suddenly looking weary. "I rest my case."

"Dad, we're not through discussing this."

"Yes, we are. For today." Christopher moved to the foot of the bed, took the woman's arm in a firm grip and guided her into the hall. "Your father isn't up to a debate. We can work out the details of his recuperation over the next few days. How long are you staying?"

"I planned to leave Monday night."

"We'll have things figured out by then. For now, your father needs rest. Short visits are best."

"What about *her?*" The woman waved a mani-cured hand toward the room.

"Marci will be leaving in a moment, too."

She adjusted her jacket and smoothed her hair. "Very well. I came straight here from the airport, and I need to freshen up, anyway. You can reach me at The Wauwinet."

Without giving him a chance to respond, she walked briskly down the hall, her heels tapping a staccato rhythm.

"Wow."

At the soft comment behind him, Christopher turned.

"You weren't kidding about her, were you?" Marci fingered the strap of her shoulder purse, faint furrows creasing her brow.

"At the risk of sounding unchristian, she's a piece of work."

"How in the world did Henry end up a with a daughter like her?"

"To hear Henry tell it, Patricia was always a social climber. He thinks it was because she saw a lot of wealth in 'Sconset among the summer people, and it made her dissatisfied with their simple lifestyle." He propped his shoulder against the wall and crossed his arms over his chest. "According to him, she set her sights on marrying into money. And she succeeded. She landed some rich guy who vacationed in 'Sconset every year with his family when he was growing up. I think she's been a great disappointment to Henry."

"Does he have any grandchildren?"

"No. Patricia is all the family he's got left."

"I overheard her mention a hotel. I take it she doesn't stay at the cottage when she visits?"

"No. It's not up to her standards." He straightened and gestured toward the room. "Let's say goodbye."

When they reentered, Henry peeked at them with one eye. "Is she gone?"

Christopher smiled. "For now."

He opened both eyes. There was less life in them now than there had been earlier, Christopher noted.

"She's gonna keep pushing for that old-folks home, you know." Henry sighed. "Too bad you never got that elder-assistance program off the ground, Christopher."

"What elder-assistance program?" Marci asked.

"Tell her about it," Henry urged.

Christopher shoved his hands into his pockets. "The concept is to set up an on-island agency that would coordinate assistance from a network of government, private and charitable groups to allow older folks who need a little help to stay in their homes. There are a lot of resources already out there, and a lot more that could be developed. I envisioned it as a largely volunteer organization supported by area churches, businesses and civic groups."

"That's a great idea."

"I told him the same thing," Henry chimed in.

His neck warmed at the praise. "Unfortunately, working out the details of the plan and then implementing it will require a lot of legwork. And I haven't had the time. It's still on the drawing board."

"Maybe someday." Henry's eyelids drifted closed.

Inclining his head toward the door, Christopher followed Marci out.

"Are you heading to the cottage now?" He paused in the hall.

"Yes."

"I left your gloves under the cushion of the rocking chair on the back porch. They should have stayed dry, despite the rain."

As they'd talked about Henry and the elder-assistance plan, the tension between them had evaporated. Now it returned full-force.

"Thanks." She edged away. "I'll see you around."

Without waiting for a reply, she headed toward the exit.

As she disappeared around a corner, Christopher followed more slowly. He needed to get to the office. His practice was growing faster than he'd expected, and he had another full patient load today. But as he walked down the hall, his mind wasn't on the colds and tick bites and sore throats and allergies he'd be treating for the rest of the day.

Instead, his thoughts were on an elderly man he'd come to love and a blonde-haired woman who was beginning to make her own inroads on his heart.

"What are you doing here?"

Startled by the sudden question after three peaceful hours in Henry's garden, with only the sound of the gulls and the surf for company, Marci spun around, scattering an armful of weeds. Patricia stood on the other side of the rose arbor. And she didn't look happy.

Planting her hands on her hips, Marci regarded the other woman. "Working in the garden."

"I can see that. My question is *why?*"

Snippy attitudes had never set well with Marci. Her chin lifted a notch. "Actually, your question was *what.* I answered that one. As for why, the garden needed tending. I offered to help Henry with it."

The woman's eyes narrowed. "How much is he paying you?"

Marci did her best to hold on to her temper. "I'm not doing it for money."

"Then what *are* you doing it for?" The woman's gaze raked over her. "And just who are you, anyway?"

Shoving her hands into her pockets, Marci balled them into fists and stared Patricia down. She ignored the first part of the question. "I'm a friend of Henry's."

Patricia's face hardened. "Do you have a key to the house?"

Given the woman's suspicious—and insulting—tone, Marci decided the question didn't merit a response. "If you'll excuse me, I have work to do." She turned her back, retrieved the rake and began to gather the scattered weeds into a pile.

Three minutes later, she heard a car engine start, followed by the sound of tires crunching on oyster shells.

The woman was gone.

Leaning on the rake, Marci took a deep breath. It was hard to believe that obnoxious woman had the same DNA as Henry. Why had she come to the cottage? To look it over with an eye to selling? According to Christopher, she'd like nothing better than to oust Henry, put the house on the market and perhaps claim an early share of her inheritance.

It might come to that someday, Marci supposed as she set the rake aside and began shoving weeds into a yard-waste bag. But it didn't have to happen now. Not if Henry had some help until he recovered.

She had three weeks left on the island, Marci mused. And lots of free time.

Much of which she intended to use to thwart Patricia's plans.

Henry was asleep when Marci stopped in at the hospital on her way home later that day, but when she approached his room the next morning, she was prepared to lay out a plan for his return to his cottage.

As she drew close, however, she heard Patricia's insistent voice echoing down the hallway.

"Dad, be reasonable. Your pension from the high school and the money you make tutoring aren't enough to get you the kind of in-home help you'll need. Face reality. You're old. You're hurt. You need to go into an assisted-living facility. It's time to sell the houses."

"I'm not leaving the cottage, Patricia."

Squaring her shoulders, Marci stepped into the room. Henry's face lit up when he saw her, and Patricia swiveled around.

Her expression was far less welcoming.

"Excuse me, Dad. I think I'll visit the ladies' room. It's getting crowded in here."

She swept toward the door, and Marci stepped aside to let her pass.

"Come on in, Marci." Henry summoned her with a weary gesture. "I'm sorry about Patricia. Her mother and I raised her better than that. But my refusal to sell the cottages has her in a snit. I never could figure out why she put such stock in the almighty dollar."

Marci pulled a chair beside the bed and sat. "I've been thinking, Henry. We'll need to see what Christopher says, but I'll be here for three more weeks. If that's long enough to get you over the hump, I'd be happy to help you out at the cottage. That way you wouldn't have to go to the assisted-living place."

Moisture glinting at the corners of his eyes, he reached out to take her hand. "That's a very generous offer, Marci."

She shrugged. "I'm at the cottage a lot anyway, working on the garden. And I'm tired of lying on the beach. We might be able to put together a plan."

His eyes brightened. "I like the idea. Let's see what Christopher says about it. I'll talk to him when he comes by later."

Patting his hand, Marci rose. "And now I'm off. That patch of weeds in the right corner is on my hit list today. You won't believe all the beautiful flowers that are emerging."

"I can't wait to see them."

"Do you need anything before I leave?"

"No. You gave me what I needed most. Hope."

With a smile, Marci stepped through the door…and found Patricia glaring at her. The woman jerked her head down the hall, indicating Marci should follow, and stalked away.

For a second, Marci considered ignoring the command. But she supposed she'd have to deal with Henry's daughter at some point. And she'd rather do it here, with other people around, than risk another encounter in the privacy of Henry's backyard.

Marci followed Patricia into the deserted waiting room, where the woman turned to her in fury.

"I heard what you said about caring for my father at the cottage. Why are you butting into his life?"

"I want what's best for him. He's my friend."

"A very *new* friend, according to my father. He told me last night you only met a couple of weeks ago. And that you're a visitor to the island who will be leaving next month. I also learned you're a waitress. Not the best-paying profession."

Folding her arms, she gave Marci's jeans and T-shirt a snooty scan. "I can see where you might be looking for a way to make an easy buck, Ms. Clay. But don't waste your time. My father might own valuable property, but he isn't wealthy. He is, however, a gullible man who tends to think the best of people and is therefore vulnerable to exploitation."

Once more her gaze raked Marci. "You never did give me a straight answer to my question yesterday. I'll ask it again. Why are you being so kind to my father?"

Reeling from the woman's implication, Marci struggled to find her tongue. "I like him."

"If you liked him, you wouldn't have let him do physical work. He's eighty-five years old. That fall could have killed him. And it wouldn't have happened if you hadn't pushed him to clean up the garden."

Blindsided by the inference, and suddenly awash with guilt, Marci didn't even notice Christopher until he appeared in the doorway of the glass-enclosed room.

"Hello, ladies."

Patricia twisted around, acknowledging his presence with a stiff dip of her head. "Doctor."

"I couldn't help overhearing some of your conversation." He stepped into the room, his demeanor grim. For the first time since they'd met, Marci saw anger in his eyes as he moved beside her in a protective stance and addressed Henry's daughter. "I can assure you, Mrs. Lawrence, that Henry was eager to restore some order to his garden. He didn't have to be pushed. But as you know, he tends to overextend himself."

"That's exactly why I want him in a place with professional oversight. I'm sure Ms. Clay's offer of assistance is very generous—" she smirked at Marci "—but I don't believe she has the appropriate medical credentials to care for my father. Do you, Doctor?"

Christopher shot Marci a look she interpreted as apologetic. "I do agree that Henry's physical well-being would be better served by a short-term stay at an extended-care facility. But if he improves as I expect him to, there's no reason he can't return to his cottage. And that will be far better for his psychological well-being long-term."

He'd nixed her plan before she could even present it, Marci realized in shock. Worse, he'd betrayed Henry.

Suddenly feeling sick to her stomach, she tightened her grip on the strap of her purse. Ignoring Patricia, she brushed past Christopher. "If you'll excuse me, I have another commitment."

Without waiting for a response, she strode down the hall.

Fighting back tears.

How could Christopher do this? He knew Henry didn't want to go into assisted living! Okay, so he *had* said it would be a short-term stay. But from what she'd seen of Patricia, she wouldn't put it past the woman to sell the cottage out from under Henry while he was away.

Spotting a ladies' room, she pushed through the door, swiping at the tears pooling in the corners of her eyes. She needed a few minutes to get herself together, muster her chutzpah.

And then she intended to give Christopher a piece of her mind.

* * *

As Christopher turned the corner in the hall where Marci had disappeared, he caught a quick glimpse of her entering the ladies' room. Slowing his pace, he stopped opposite the door, leaned back against the wall and shoved his hands into his pockets. Although he'd promised to join Patricia in her father's room to discuss the next steps, Marci was his top priority. The look of betrayal in her eyes before she'd practically run down the hall had been like a punch in the gut.

Three minutes later, when the door opened and she emerged, he straightened up.

She saw him at once, and the mutinous tilt of her chin told him this was going to be a hard sell.

"I expected you to be busy with Patricia arranging Henry's move to assisted living."

He took her arm. "We need to talk." Without giving her a chance to respond, he tugged her toward a door marked private.

He knew his surprise move was the only reason he was able to propel her into the supply room. Once inside, he closed the door and stood in front of it.

Bright spots of color appeared on her cheeks as she faced off against him, her antagonism almost palpable. And the redness around her eyes told him she'd been crying.

"I'm not selling Henry out, Marci."

She glared at him. "You could have fooled me. You know he doesn't want to go to assisted living! You said yourself he'd wither and die in a place like that, just like your grandfather did."

"That's true. But I also saw the results of his latest tests this morning. His blood count isn't rebounding as quickly as we'd like. And he's having a lot more discomfort than he's letting on to visitors. That should all improve. But it will take a while. And for the first week or so, I'll feel more comfortable if he's got round-the-clock care from medical professionals. After that, assuming we can arrange for some home help for him, there's no reason he can't return to the cottage."

"If his daughter doesn't sell it in the meantime."

Christopher fixed her with a steady look. "She can't do that. I have his power of attorney."

He knew the instant she grasped the implication—that Henry trusted Christopher more than he did his own daughter—because the tension in both her features and her stance eased subtly.

"Okay." She blew out a long breath. "I guess I overreacted. Sorry."

"Don't apologize for caring." He gentled his tone as he reached over to brush away a streak of mascara from her cheek. "His daughter could take a few lessons from you."

His fingers lingered on her skin, and for a long moment their gazes locked. He saw a quick flash of emotion—strong enough to stop him in his tracks—before she took a jerky step back and swiped at her eyes.

"I just…" She stopped. Swallowed. "I just don't like to see people being used."

The sudden hard edge to her words raised Christopher's antennas, but she continued before he could follow-up.

"Besides, as Patricia pointed out, if I hadn't convinced him to fix up the garden, this wouldn't have happened."

Her voice got husky, and she blinked away a new batch of tears.

A muscle clenched in his jaw, and his anger surged again, as it had when he'd discovered Patricia berating Marci. The caring woman standing inches away deserved gratitude, not insults. "Henry's been wanting to clean it out for a long time. He was thrilled when you offered to help. Don't let her make you feel guilty about that."

Tempted to once again touch her face, he shoved his hand in his pocket instead. "I overheard some of the rest of what she said, too. Including her insinuation about your motives. That comment was more indicative of her character than yours, Marci. Don't let it bother you." He propped a shoulder against the closed door, wanting to extend this private moment as long as possible. "Are you headed to Henry's?"

"That was my plan." She fished a tissue out of her pocket and swiped at her nose. "But with this new turn of events, I think I'll go back to The Devon Rose and see if I can get on Heather's computer. As part of my last social-work practicum, I got some experience finding assistance for seniors. I'd like to search the net and see what I can come up with for Henry. I'd also like to take a look at your elder-assistance plan sometime, if you don't mind. It might give me some ideas."

"I'll be happy to share it, although it's rough. I keep it at my office." He folded his arms across his chest. "You know, our office manager isn't there on Saturdays. You could come by and not only get the plan, but do some research on her computer."

"Are you sure I wouldn't disrupt anything?"

Only his heart.

"No. This will work out fine. Let me finish up with Henry, and I'll meet you there in about fifteen minutes. It's easy to find." He pulled out a prescription pad, jotted down the directions and tore off the sheet.

She took it from his outstretched hand and tucked it in the pocket of her jeans. "Okay."

When he didn't move away from the door at once, she gave him an expectant look. One that contained both trepidation and a whisper of yearning.

Henry had been telling him for months that he needed to move on. Maybe it was finally time.

Even though he suspected Marci had secrets, perhaps they weren't deal breakers, as Denise's had been. Perhaps…

"Christopher?"

At Marci's question, he moved away from the door. Now wasn't the time or place to explore that possibility. "Sorry. I'll see you in a few minutes."

She edged past him without meeting his eyes and took off down the hall.

As he watched her walk away, he found himself again comparing her to the woman who had soured him on romance. And the differences were obvious. Denise had used tears to get what she wanted; Marci did her best to hide hers. Denise had been needy; Marci reached out to those in need. She was also smart, intelligent, spunky, kind, attractive.

So why hadn't some guy claimed her by now?

Was it because the secret she harbored had given her an aversion to romance?

Christopher didn't know the answer to that question. But he knew he needed to find it before she boarded the plane back to Chicago in three weeks.

Chapter Eight

This was really good stuff.

As Marci finished reviewing Christopher's notes on his elder-assistance program, she leaned back in the office manager's chair, impressed. Although he'd claimed to have done little, that wasn't quite true. He'd made a number of contacts in the community, and his idea had been met with a positive response. He'd compiled a list of contacts yet to be tapped. And he'd researched some of the services already available to seniors on Nantucket. It was an excellent start.

Setting aside the file containing his notes, Marci began browsing the Net. In short order, she located several additional resources for seniors that sounded worthy of investigation, and she found some interesting articles about new programs sprouting up around the country designed around the philosophy of keeping older citizens in their homes.

She'd filled several pages with scribbled ideas and Web sites that merited further exploration when the receptionist appeared in the doorway of the small office.

"Sorry to interrupt. I wanted to let you know we'll be closing at one. I thought you might need a few minutes to wrap up."

Marci checked her watch. Where had the past three hours gone? "Thanks. I'm about done, anyway. Would you like me to shut down the computer?"

"I'll take care of it. And don't feel you have to rush. Dr. Morgan still has a patient in the waiting room. You've got a few more minutes."

"Okay. Thanks."

Left alone again, Marci jotted some notes about an innovative time-bank idea, then tapped the sheets into a pile, slung her purse over her shoulder and picked up Christopher's file.

The receptionist was back at her desk when Marci emerged. The woman looked up as she approached, smiling as she gestured to the file. "It's a great idea, isn't it?"

Uncertain how much Christopher had shared with his office staff, Marci erred on the side of caution in her response. "Yes. It could help a lot of people."

"My own grandmother, for one. She's seventy-nine and has lived in the same house since she got married fifty-eight years ago. But it's getting to be too much for her to manage. I know she'd—"

A baby's wail pierced the air from the direction of the waiting room just as one of the examining-room doors opened. A smock-clad nurse with salt-and-pepper hair stepped into the hall, closing the door behind her.

"I take it Mrs. Anderson is here." She grinned at the receptionist as she approached.

"With brood in tow." The woman rolled her eyes.

Walking to the door, the nurse ushered in a young mother who was bouncing the screaming baby. The toddler clinging to her skirt gave the adults in the office a wary inspection.

"Let's get your weight." The nurse doubled her volume to be heard above the howling baby and indicated the scale in the hall near the reception desk.

The diaper bag began to slip off the mother's shoulder, and she tried to shrug it back into place as the baby gave another piercing wail. Spotting Marci, she homed in on her.

"Would you mind holding my baby while I get weighed?" She flashed her a flustered grin. "I don't need the extra fourteen pounds."

Before Marci could protest, she placed the flailing infant in her arms.

As the squirming little body settled against her chest, Marci stared down at the scrunched-up face.

And tried to breathe.

"Here, let me take that stuff." The receptionist stood and leaned over the desk, tugging Christopher's file and Marci's notes from her hand. "Isn't she a cutie?" She reached over and touched the baby's nose, but the infant slapped her hand away.

"I see she has a temper to go with those red curls." The woman chuckled.

"Danny, let go of Mommy's skirt. She has to get on the scale." The mother was still trying to disengage from her toddler, Marci noted in desperation.

Though her arms felt stiff, she instinctively began to bounce the screaming infant.

"This baby is one of Dr. Morgan's special children," the receptionist commented as she rested her arms on the counter and regarded the little bundle.

Marci's throat tightened at the pleasurable feeling of the tiny warm body against her chest. "What do you mean?"

"He's very active in the pro-life movement. Mrs. Anderson couldn't have any more children after Danny, but she wanted another baby. Dr. Morgan has connections with Birthright in Boston, and he helped arrange an adoption."

Marci's stomach clenched, and she felt a film of sweat break out on her upper lip.

"Now that's amazing. You must have the touch."

At the receptionist's comment, Marci gave her a blank look.

The woman gestured to the child in her arms. "Peace reigns once again."

The room had gone silent, Marci realized as she looked down. The infant was staring up at her with big blue eyes, one fist jammed in her mouth. With the other hand, she grabbed a handful of Marci's T-shirt and hiccupped.

As Marci focused on the diminutive fist, tears formed in her eyes. Each finger was so tiny, yet so perfect.

Just like—

A door opened down the hall, and a white-coated Christopher joined the small group gathered by the receptionist's desk.

Struggling to breathe in the suddenly airless room, Marci moved toward him. "I have to go." She pushed the baby against his chest.

He frowned, but to her relief he automatically lifted his arms. Once she knew the baby was secure, she turned away and rushed to the door, fumbling with the knob.

"Marci, wait a second. What's the—"

She didn't wait to hear the rest of Christopher's question. Pushing through the door, she dashed across the empty waiting room and practically ran to her car.

As she fitted the key into the ignition, she could only imagine the reaction of the adults she'd left behind. They probably thought her behavior was bizarre.

But it wasn't. Not if you knew the reason behind it. Only two people were privy to that secret, however.

And Marci had no intention of revealing it to anyone else.

As Christopher approached 'Sconset, he eased back on the accelerator. He'd intended to visit Henry again after finishing at the office. But Marci's hasty departure—and distraught expression—had changed his plans.

Although he'd probed, his receptionist had been unable to offer any clues about what had upset her. In fact, she'd said they'd had a pleasant exchange only a few minutes before.

Yet something had unnerved her.

He didn't know if she'd followed through on her plan to go to Henry's once she finished at his office. But he had a feeling she might have. His neighbor's garden would give her a nice, quiet place to think through whatever had upset her.

As he pulled onto Henry's street, he spotted her car parked near the arbor in the older man's backyard. Good. His hunch had been right.

Easing the car to a stop in front of his cottage, he entered through the front door and strode toward his tiny kitchenette. From the window, he could see Marci attacking the weeds next door with a vengeance. As if she was still distressed—or angry.

Although she sidestepped most personal questions with practiced ease, he intended to do his best to find out what was bothering her. Because he wanted to help, if he could. That's what you did for friends. Especially friends who were beginning to become much more.

Five minutes later, after exchanging his work clothes for jeans and a T-shirt, he picked up the elder-assistance file and the notes she'd left in his office. Exiting through the back door, he approached the white picket fence that separated the two yards and sent a silent prayer heavenward.

Lord, give me the words that will reach her heart.

Pausing at the fence, he drew in a steadying breath. "Could you use some help?"

At his question, Marci swung toward him, hoe frozen midstrike.

"I thought you said you were going to do rounds after office hours?"

"I changed my mind. I'm filling in for half a shift in the E.R. tonight, so I'll visit patients before that." He waved the file and papers at her. "You left these behind."

A soft blush crept over her cheeks as she set the hoe aside and approached him.

"Sorry." She reached across the fence to take them.

He tightened his grip as she tugged. "Before I hand these over, do you want to tell me what happened back at the office?"

She retracted her hand and tucked it in her pocket. "What do you mean?"

"You know what I mean."

Moistening her lips, she lifted one shoulder and adopted a nonchalance too deliberate to be authentic. "I was still thinking about the encounter with Henry's daughter."

He didn't buy that. She was hiding something. But maybe if he could put her at ease, she'd drop a few clues.

Passing over the material, he vaulted the fence. Marci's eyes widened, and she immediately took several steps back.

"Patricia can do that to a person. I had to bite my tongue more than once while she and I and Henry discussed his recuperation plans."

"How did he take the news about going to the assisted-living place?"

"Not well. I hope when we talk one-on-one he'll realize it's for the best in the short-term."

"Good luck."

"Yeah. So…" He scanned the yard. "Tell me where you could use an extra pair of hands."

Depositing her notes and the file on the rocking chair in the corner of the porch, she sent him a wary look. "You seriously want to help in the garden?"

"Sure. It's too nice a day to waste indoors."

Skepticism narrowed her eyes. "Do you know how to tell weeds and flowers apart?"

"I think so. With a little coaching."

"Okay. I'm working on that section this afternoon." She gestured to the long expanse by the fence on the far side of the yard.

"Lead the way."

He followed, enjoying the way her springy blond curls bounced when she walked. The view of her trim figure wasn't too shabby, either. And he liked the way long hours in the sun had brought out a few freckles on her porcelain complexion. Just a mere sprinkling across the bridge of her nose.

"Well?"

Christopher came out of his reverie and realized she'd asked him a question.

"Sorry. I was, uh, thinking about how sunny it is. With your fair skin, you should be wearing a hat."

"I use a lot of sunscreen." She pointed to a section of the garden. "Do you want to start here?"

"Yeah. That's fine."

"If you have any questions, just ask. I don't want you pulling up half of Henry's flowers."

She moved a few feet down, dropped to her knees, and dove into the soil again.

Following her example, Christopher got up close and personal with the garden. Not until then did he realize just how overgrown it was.

"Wow. This is a mess."

"Tell me about it."

He started yanking out weeds. "Are you sorry you took on the challenge?"

"No. I've never liked neglected gardens. They make me sad, for some reason. It feels good to give the flowers an environment where they can thrive and bloom."

"You're making great progress." A quick glance around the garden showed she was three-fourths of the way through.

"It's coming along. I want it to be done when Henry comes home." She shoved her hair back from her face, leaving an endearing streak of dirt on her cheek. "I was impressed with your elder-assistance plan, by the way."

"It needs a lot of work."

"You've laid a good foundation, though. And you've identified a lot of potential supporters and resources. I like the idea of a talent-exchange registry. It would offer services not available through existing programs like meals-on-wheels and the island shuttle service."

He gently extricated a daisy from a tangle of greenery and began pulling up the weeds that were choking it. "It seems to have potential. But it's not a new concept. Bartering has been around for ages. This just formalizes it a little. For example, Henry taught English for years. He could easily help someone polish their résumé, or review a college-application essay, or help draft a grant for a local nonprofit organization. They, in turn, could paint his house. Or weed his garden. Or run errands."

"Building on that idea, I read about some groups that are also doing time banks, where seniors help each other," Marci said. "For every hour they help someone else—whether it's caring for a pet, grocery shopping, changing light bulbs, raking leaves, you name it—they bank hours they can redeem for help when they need it."

He looked over at her. She'd stopped pulling weeds, and her eyes were sparkling with enthusiasm.

She was the most gorgeous woman he'd ever seen.

"What I like best about those kinds of approaches is that no one feels like they're relying on charity or taking advantage of someone else, you know?" She sat back on her heels, her expression earnest. "We could even pull in young people. Maybe for each half hour they volunteer, they could earn points redeemable for merchandise or movies or food donated by area businesses. Plus, I think interaction between seniors and young people would be a good thing. Older folks have a lot to offer."

"That all sounds great, Marci. But coordinating it is a huge time commitment. That's why it's never gotten off the ground."

She surveyed the garden. "I'll have this done in another few days. I could at least get the ball rolling while I'm lining up resources for Henry. That is, if you'd like me to. It's your program."

"The idea may have started with me, but it needs someone to take it forward. The way things are going, I'm never going to have the time to make it a reality."

"Okay." She went back to work. "I'll start by getting in touch with some of the contacts you listed. Any suggestions on who to talk to first?"

"Reverend Kaizer at my church would be good. I mentioned the idea to him months ago, and he was very supportive. Plus, he's well-connected on the island. He could put you in touch with a lot of people who might be willing to help get this thing launched. I could introduce you to him if you'd like to join me for services tomorrow."

In his peripheral vision, he saw her freeze for an instant before she resumed tugging at a stubborn weed. "I'm not a churchgoer. God and I have never communicated much."

At her poignant tone, Christopher sent her a speculative look. "It sounds like you wish that would change."

She rubbed her palms on her jeans, leaving streaks of dirt on the fabric. "Sometimes. J.C. finds great solace in his faith. Even my other brother, who was never very interested in religion, has embraced the whole concept. But I'm not sure." She tucked her hair behind her ear and kept her face averted. "Let's just say I'm not exactly a role model for Christianity."

"I find that hard to believe."

"Believe it."

He thought about pushing, but had learned to recognize that firm set of her jaw as a sign to back off.

"Well, no matter why you believe that, I can promise that you'd be welcome at services. And it would give you a chance to meet Reverend Kaiser."

There was silence for a few moments as she dug in the fertile earth.

"I'll think about it, okay?"

"Sure." At least she hadn't refused outright. "Is this ferny stuff a flower?"

She crawled closer to inspect it. Close enough for him to get a whiff of her sweet scent. Close enough to feel the warmth emanating from her body. Close enough to find himself fighting the impulse to lift his hand and touch those golden curls.

"That's an astilbe. They get colored plumes later in the summer. Or so Henry tells me."

She crawled back and resumed her work.

For the next hour, they spoke little. Christopher tried a couple of times to start another conversation, but Marci didn't cooperate. At last, after checking his watch, he rose.

"I need to have some dinner and take care of a few things before I head back to town."

She stood as well, brushing off the knees of her jeans. "I'm about to wrap up for the day, too."

After they stored the garden tools in Henry's shed, Marci went to retrieve her purse and the file and notes from the chair on the porch.

"I'm going to go home and change." She dug in her purse and withdrew her keys. "Would you tell Henry I'll stop by later?"

"Sure. Let me give you my cell number. You can call and let me know what you decide about church. I'll have my phone with me in the E.R."

Once more she opened her purse, rummaging for a pen and paper. As he recited the number, she jotted it down. "Okay. Thanks for helping."

"No problem." He looked over the fence at the back of Henry's property, where grass gave way to sand and the sea sparkled in the sun. "It was nice to have an excuse to spend time outside on such a beautiful day."

And with such a beautiful woman, he added in silence when he turned back to find a winsome smile tugging at Marci's lips as she, too, admired the view.

"Yeah. This spot feels like a little piece of heaven."

Only one thing could make it better, Christopher thought as he regarded Marci in the golden afternoon light.

"Well, I better be off. See you later." With a wave, she headed for the gate.

A couple of minutes later, he heard her car pull away from the cottage. And as the sound receded into the distance, leaving quiet in its wake, only the pounding of the surf, and of his pulse, disturbed the tranquility around—and inside—him.

Chapter Nine

This was a mistake.

As Marci flipped through the small closet in her cottage, trying to decide what to wear to church, she was having serious second thoughts about agreeing to attend. She didn't belong in a house of God.

On the other hand, she did want to meet the minister. Christopher had said the man was enthusiastic about the elder-assistance idea, and if she was going to pull anything together in the short time she had left on the island, she needed a lot of help. And the sooner the better.

The Lord would just have to put up with her for one day.

Pulling a beige skirt and a cotton madras blouse off their hangars, she tossed them on the bed as a knock sounded at the door.

Her pulse took a leap, and she checked her watch.

Christopher was twenty minutes early. And she wasn't anywhere close to ready!

"Marci?" Another, more persistent knock. "You there?"

She sagged against the wall. J.C.

Relieved, she padded over to the door and pulled it open.

Her brother grinned as he eyed her baggy sleep shirt, tousled curls and bare feet. "Did I wake you?"

"It's eight-thirty. Only slugs sleep this late."

"Hey, it's okay to sleep in on vacation. Although this hasn't been much of one for you, from what I can see."

"I like keeping busy."

"That's not what vacation is supposed to be all about."

At his chiding tone, she folded her arms across her chest and gave him a pointed look. "To each his own. So, what's up?"

"A little prickly this morning, aren't we?"

She chose not to dignify that comment with a reply. Instead, she arched an eyebrow and shot him a disparaging look—a well-practiced stance that discouraged most men.

But it didn't work with her brother. It never had.

Chuckling, he propped a shoulder against the doorframe. "You know, I love you even when you're in one of these ornery moods. Anyway, Heather and I are going to brunch after church.

Want to join us? We could swing back around and pick you up."

Uh-oh. She hadn't told him about her plans for the morning, intending to simply walk into church and surprise him. That way, he'd have the whole service to recover from his shock at her presence. And if she was lucky, Heather would rein in the interrogation that was sure to follow.

"Um, I'm not sure that will work."

"Why not? We'll have the car, so you can't go anywhere. You might as well eat with us."

She was stuck. He'd keep pushing until she gave him a reasonable explanation for her refusal.

Taking a deep breath, she plunged in. "I don't know what my plans will be after church, J.C. I'm going to the service with Christopher."

Her brother's astonished expression was almost comical. "You're going to church?"

"Yeah."

"With Christopher Morgan? Henry's neighbor?"

"Yeah."

He squinted at her. "Why?"

"It's a chance to meet the minister. He's interested in helping get the elder-assistance program I told you about off the ground. And that will be good for Henry." She checked her watch. "Look, he's going to be here in a few minutes. I need to get ready."

She started to close the door, but J.C.'s hand shot out and grabbed the edge. "Not so fast. You can't drop a bombshell like that and then shut the door. I've been trying for years to get you to go to church. Yet the first time the good doctor invites you, you accept. How come I think there's more to this than helping Henry?"

"Because you have a suspicious and cynical mind honed by years of detective work among the dregs of Chicago humanity." She shook the door. "Let it go, J.C. And I'm talking about more than the door."

He ignored her. "Am I sensing a touch of romance here?" A grin once more tugged at his lips. "I can't remember the last time I saw you blush."

"Just because you're a newlywed does not mean others share your interest in all that mushy stuff," she said through clenched teeth, ruing the telltale warmth in her cheeks.

"Sounds like a certain 'Sconset doctor might."

She clamped her lips together, jerked the door free and slammed it in his face.

Much to her dismay, she heard his muted laughter on the other side of the door.

"For the record, I'm all for it," he called. "Assuming he's a good guy, of course."

"Goodbye, J.C."

Another chuckle. "See you at church."

The sound of his off-key whistling floated in through the open window as he headed back down the flagstone path toward Lighthouse Lane.

Stomping into the bathroom, Marci rummaged

through her makeup kit and twisted the cap off her mascara. Talk about overbearing big brothers!

He was reading way too much into this church visit, she assured herself as she added a touch of blush, applied some lipstick and returned to the main room. Christopher's only reason for suggesting they attend services together was to introduce her to the minister. There had been nothing personal about the invitation.

Not true, a little voice whispered in her mind. *A simple phone call to the minister would have sufficed as an introduction. He invited you for the same reason you accepted.*

She had to face reality.

While she'd consented to accompany Christopher on the pretext of implementing his plan and helping Henry, the primary drive behind her decision had been her attraction to the blue-eyed doctor with the compassionate heart.

And after that moment in the garden when he'd almost kissed her, she knew the feeling was mutual.

That was the truth. Straight-up. And ignoring it wasn't going to change anything. She needed to confront the situation head-on and with absolute honesty. That was the best way to deal with it.

However, that honesty did not have to extend to her brother, she decided as she smoothed her skirt over her hips.

Because the last thing she needed in her life was another matchmaker.

* * *

As the pianist played the introduction for the final hymn, Christopher sent Marci a discreet glance. Each time he'd checked on her, she'd appeared to be engaged in the service. She'd listened with rapt attention to Reverend Kaizer, who had used the story of Mary Magdalene to illustrate the theme of forgiveness in his sermon. She'd followed along in the hymnal, though she hadn't joined in the singing. She'd closed her eyes a few times during the readings, as if contemplating the words of scripture.

Although she'd seemed a bit on edge when he'd picked her up, her expression now was serene, suggesting she'd found the experience worthwhile.

And that was good. For a lot of reasons—some of which were personal. It had always been important to him that any woman he dated share his basic beliefs.

But this wasn't a date, he reminded himself.

Even if he wished it was.

The hymn ended, and Christopher stepped out of the pew. When Marci exited behind him, he took her arm and guided her toward the back of church.

"What did you think?"

"It was interesting. I didn't expect to leave with such a peaceful feeling. Is it like that for you?"

"Every Sunday."

As they joined the groups of congregants gathering on the church lawn, Edith waved to them.

Taking Chester's arm, she tugged him in their direction.

"Well, isn't this cozy!" She beamed at them as she drew close. "I didn't realize you two were so well-acquainted."

Christopher sent Marci a quick look, noted the pink tinge on her cheeks and diverted the conversation to a less personal topic. "Marci's doing some development work on that elder-assistance program I mentioned to you a few months ago. She might need to tap into your network of contacts."

"Glad to help. Sounds like a worthwhile effort. What got you interested?" she asked Marci.

"Henry Calhoun, Christopher's neighbor. He had a fall, and he'll be needing some assistance once he goes home. I met him when he came to tea, and we hit it off."

"I heard about Henry's accident from a friend who works at the hospital. Don't know him well myself, but our paths have crossed a few times. Nice man. You've met him, haven't you, Chester?"

"Yep."

Christopher took Marci's arm—a propriety gesture not lost on Edith, judging by the sudden twinkle in the older woman's eye. He hoped Marci hadn't noticed. She was skittish enough already. "If you'll excuse us, I want to introduce Marci to Reverend Kaizer. He'll be another good resource for the program."

"By all means. Grab him while he has a free minute. See you both later." With a flutter of fingers, Edith headed toward another cluster of people, Chester trotting along a few steps behind.

A rueful grin playing at his lips, Christopher shook his head. "To use an old cliché, I don't think any grass grows under her feet."

"No kidding."

"Let's catch Reverend Kaizer before someone else corners him."

Five minutes later, after a conversation that included setting up an appointment for Marci to meet with the man early in the week, they strolled side-by-side across the grass toward his car.

"I stopped in to see Henry on my way to pick you up."

"I'm planning to visit him later. How is he?"

"Improving. When I left, he was trying to convince Patricia to go home early."

She gave him a wry smile "I can't say I blame him. She's—"

"Marci!"

At the summons, they stopped. Marci's brother and his wife were approaching, and Christopher thought he detected a quiet sigh from the woman beside him.

J.C. stuck out his hand, and Christopher took it in a firm grip. As the two men exchanged a greeting, he recognized the protective look in J.C.'s eyes.

Marci's brother was sizing him up. Interesting. It seemed Edith and Henry weren't the only ones picking up the vibes between him and the lovely lady beside him.

"Hello, Heather." He smiled at the elegant woman with the light brown hair.

She tucked her hand in her husband's arm with an amused smile. "Nice to see you, Christopher."

"Marci, I wanted to check with you on the brunch. You never did say what your plans were for after church." J.C. gave Christopher a speculative perusal.

"If it's okay, I thought I might borrow Heather's computer and do a little work on the elder-assistance plan."

His gaze whipped back to her, and he frowned. "You're not supposed to work on Sunday. This should be a day of rest and relaxation and fun." J.C. directed another glance his way, and Christopher recognized the hint.

So did Marci.

And she didn't like it.

Stepping closer to her brother, she fixed him with a narrow-eyed glare. "I don't have a lot of time left here, J.C., and I want to make some progress on the plan. In fact, if you don't mind, you and Heather can drop me off at the house on your way to eat and save Christopher a trip."

"I don't mind taking you home," Christopher chimed in.

She turned to him with a smile that seemed pasted on. "Thank you. But this is more practical."

And it also sent a clear message to her brother, he acknowledged. Back off. Butt out. Don't push.

A grin twitched at Heather's lips, and she moved closer to her husband. "We'll be happy to run you home, Marci. Right, J.C.?"

He gave his sister a disgruntled scowl, clearly not pleased with the outcome of the conversation.

"Thanks, Heather." Marci sent the other woman a grateful look before she addressed him. "I'll see you around, Christopher. Thanks for introducing me to Reverend Kaizer."

"My pleasure."

Linking her arm with her brother's, Marci propelled him toward the car. Flanked by the two women, J.C. had no option except to follow.

Christopher shoved his hands into his pockets and watched them walk away, a grin of admiration tugging at his lips. Marci Clay was one feisty woman. If her deft handling of her brother was any indication, very few people managed to outmaneuver her.

"Lovely girl, isn't she?"

He shifted around to find Edith once more approaching. "Yes, she is. With a very protective brother."

"J.C. feels a lot of responsibility for his siblings. He raised them after their mother died, you know."

"I heard part of that story."

"He just wants what's best for Marci."

"I can understand that."

She nodded in approval. "In that case, you and he will hit it off fine. Well, it's off to The Flake and some sugar doughnuts for us. I'll talk to Marci later today and see how I can help with that plan of yours."

Signaling to Chester, who was talking to another older man across the lawn, she headed toward the parking area.

As Christopher ambled back to his own car, he replayed Edith's comment about J.C. wanting what was best for Marci. He did, too.

The question was, what *was* best for her?

Based on the message she'd just sent her brother, it was clear she didn't think it was a relationship between them. And he would have agreed with that conclusion until a few days ago.

Now he wasn't as certain it was true.

For her…or for him.

She was finished.

Wiping her hands on her jeans, Marci stepped up onto Henry's back porch and surveyed the yard. After nine days of hard work, the garden lining three sides of the fence looked pristine. The myriad of flowers lovingly planted by Henry's wife had been revealed, and though she didn't know many of their names, Marci appreciated the blending of heights and colors and textures that spoke of careful planning and an eye for beauty.

Today marked another milestone, too. Henry was leaving the hospital for the rehab facility.

She'd taken to calling it that, hoping it would reinforce the temporary nature of his stay. But the older man still wasn't happy about it. He wanted to come home. Sooner rather than later.

The one bright spot was that his daughter had gone. Meaning his life was much more peaceful.

Gathering up the heavy-duty gardening tools for the last time, Marci glanced over at Christopher's cottage as she lugged them toward the storage shed. Since their trip to church three days ago, she'd made a conscious effort to avoid him. No sense adding more fuel to the fire. Both Edith and J.C. had been peppering her with questions about their relationship. Edith had taken the subtle approach, always prefaced by the delivery of some sweet treat to her cottage. J.C. had been much more direct.

Neither tactic had elicited any additional information, however. As her peeved brother had remarked, she'd closed up as tight as a Nantucket quahog.

And she wasn't about to open up anytime soon, she resolved, stowing the rake and hoe in the corner of the shed. What was the point? There was no future in a relationship between her and Christopher.

Besides the fact that she was only a visitor to the island, their backgrounds were too different. He was a doctor. She was an unemployed social worker. He came from wealth. His family had vacationed on pricey Nantucket every year—for *three* weeks. Her idea of vacation was an El ride to the lake with a sack lunch on a rare free Sunday afternoon. Plus, given his love for children and his support of the pro-life movement, he'd be totally turned off if he knew about the tragic mistakes she'd made.

Steering clear of him was the sensible thing to do, she assured herself as she secured the shed door.

That's why she was timing her garden work and visits to Henry during hours when she knew Christopher was seeing patients. The remainder of the day, she worked on his plan. It was coming along very well and had elicited an enthusiastic response from all the contacts she'd made. If it continued to progress as she hoped, she was confident it would be ready to implement by the time she left.

Plus, as she finessed the plan, she was also rounding up all the resources Henry would need after he came home to his cottage.

Her sojourn on Nantucket had been productive in a lot of ways, she thought, fingering the soiled leather garden gloves that had protected her hands from unexpected thorns as she'd toiled in Henry's garden.

Too bad she hadn't had some way to protect her heart as well.

Because thanks to a certain Nantucket doctor, a piece of it would remain behind when she returned to Chicago, leaving an empty place that she suspected would never be filled again.

Chapter Ten

On Thursday afternoon, Marci rounded the corner in the hall at the rehab center—and came face-to-face with Christopher.

As she stumbled back in surprise, his hand shot out to steady her. "Sorry."

In the second it took her to regain her balance, the timing of his visit registered. His presence in the middle of office hours didn't bode well.

Her breath caught in her throat as her pulse accelerated. "Is Henry okay?"

He frowned. "He's running a slight temperature. There's a little inflammation around the incision, which could be the cause. But with his compromised immune system, we're being aggressive with antibiotics."

"It must be serious or you wouldn't have interrupted office hours."

"I had a no-show. That gave me a window to run over. I think he'll be fine, but we'll be keeping a close eye on him."

"Is he up to a visitor?"

The furrows on his brow eased, and one side of his mouth hitched up into a smile—which did nothing to calm her pulse. "If her name is Patricia, no. If her name is Marci, yes. I had to promise not to tell his daughter about this glitch, by the way."

"I can understand that."

"Me, too." He checked his watch. "I need to run. Go on in. Your visit will cheer him up. His spirits could use a little boost today."

"Okay." She handed him the file that was tucked under her arm. "I was going to leave this with Henry and ask him to pass it on to you, but you might as well as take it with you. It's a semifinal draft of your plan. Before I go any further, I wanted to get your reaction. See you later."

Continuing down the hall, she restrained the urge to look back and see if Christopher was watching her. And hoped the visit with Henry would distract her from thoughts of the blue-eyed doctor.

It did. But not in a good way.

Since she'd stopped by yesterday, he seemed to have aged ten years. He was lying down rather than sitting up as he had been when they'd chatted less than twenty-four hours ago, and his cheeks were sunken and flushed.

Yet when his eyelids flickered open and he saw her, he managed a weary smile. "Hello, Marci. Come to visit an old man, I see."

Adopting a bright tone, she walked into the room. "No. I came to visit one of the most youthful men I know."

"In spirit, maybe. Too bad the body can't keep up."

She didn't like his attitude. It held a hint of surrender she'd never heard from him before.

"I saw Christopher in the hallway." She drew up a chair beside the bed. "He told me you have slight temperature, but he didn't seem overly concerned. As far as I know, you're still on track to ditch this place sometime next week."

He brushed his gnarled fingers over the sheet that covered him. "Maybe."

"Henry Calhoun!" Marci gave him a look of mock indignation and took his hand in a firm grip. "After all the work I've done to put a whole army of resources at your disposal, you better plan on marching out this door next week. Meals-on-wheels, a personal shopper, rides to medical appointments, pharmacy deliveries…you name it. Besides, I'm missing your banana-nut bread."

Her attempt at humor brought a fleeting smile to his lips. "I'm kind of missing that myself." He patted her hand. "We'll see, Marci. Let's take it a day at a time."

He was giving up. Marci could hear it his voice. See it in his resigned expression. Feel it in his consoling pat of her hand.

"Henry." She leaned close, her posture intent. "You *are* going to get better. You can't let Patricia win."

He peered at her and pursed his lips. "That *would* be a shame, wouldn't it?"

"You bet. You have a lot of good years left. At home, in your cottage. I finished the garden, by the way. I can't wait for you to see it. In fact, why don't we plan a picnic dinner out there your first night back?"

"I'd like that."

She stood and leaned down to press a kiss to his too-warm forehead. "We have a date, then. And I don't like being stood up. Can I count on you to be there?"

He smiled. "I'll do my best."

"Good. I'll be back later tonight. How about I bring you some of those chocolate tarts you liked at tea?"

"They sure were tasty."

"Done. I'll raid Heather's kitchen. Get some rest this afternoon, okay?"

"Not much else I can do. Take care, Marci."

Exiting the room, she quickly retraced her steps down the hall. While the place was well-kept, and colorful Fourth of July decorations brightened the common rooms in anticipation of the coming holiday, she always felt an oppressive sense of gloom as she passed the residents hunched in wheelchairs or shuffling along behind walkers.

She couldn't think of a more depressing place to live.

Christopher was right. Henry would wither and die here. They had to get him out as soon as possible.

And in the meantime, she had to think of some way to give him an incentive to keep fighting.

But where could she turn for inspiration?

God.

The word echoed in her mind, resonating powerfully enough to make her step falter for an instant.

Where in the world had that come from?

It had been years since she'd prayed. Or even *thought* about praying. But she *had* attended a service last Sunday and observed a lot people who put great stock in prayer.

She picked up her pace again. Maybe this might be one of the situations where prayer could make a difference. It had done the trick with Nathan last year, when she and J.C. had visited him in his darkest hour.

What did she have to lose?

Stepping out into the sunlight, Marci stopped, drew a deep, cleansing breath of the fresh Nantucket air and closed her eyes.

Lord, I have no idea if You're listening. I kind of doubt it, since we haven't exactly been on speaking terms. But if You are, could You help my friend, Henry? He's a good man, Lord. And I don't think he's ready to check out yet. But he needs some encouragement. Please lift up his spirits. And help me think of something that will make him realize how much he's loved and how much we want him to get better.

And Lord, if I've got Your ear, thank You for bringing such two special men into my world. Henry's like the grandfather I never had, and Christopher…well, I don't know where he fits in. But I do know he's a remarkable man. And no matter what happens, meeting him has been one of the greatest gifts of my life.

Wow.

Christopher flipped over the last page of the plan Marci had put together and took a sip of his cooling coffee. She'd done a fabulous job weaving a bunch of random ideas into a coherent proposal. Her plan relied on contributions from area residents, businesses, churches and organizations, and she'd already lined up an impressive level of funding commitments and support. Plus, she'd compiled a comprehensive database of volunteers willing to assist with the effort or participate in the time bank. And the high-school administration had embraced the notion of youth involvement and promised to promote it.

The plan was also very professional—well-organized, well-thought-out and well-presented. The rationale was compelling, the payback to the community clearly outlined.

Rising from the kitchen table in his cottage, he rinsed his mug in the sink. There was only one thing he might change in Marci's proposal. She'd suggested the organization be run by a volunteer committee. But based on the comprehensive nature and scale of the coordination required for it to function effectively, it needed a more formalized structure. And an office.

Months ago, when he'd mentioned the idea to a few people at the hospital, word had spread to top management. And a casual comment had been made by one of the executives about donating office space. He made a mental note to follow up on that first thing tomorrow.

As for structure—Marci's program deserved a full-time, professional director. It needed to be run by someone with credentials in social service work and an affinity for the elderly.

In other words, someone like Marci.

Or better yet, Marci herself.

Would she be willing to stay? he wondered. More importantly, did he have the courage to *ask* her to stay?

As he mulled that over, he pushed through the back door into the deepening twilight. Ambling across the lawn, he surveyed Henry's garden over the white picket fence. Order had been restored, and the plants and flowers were once more reaching for the sky, free to bloom now that they'd been liberated from the choking weeds.

Henry would be pleased.

And if he were standing here now, Christopher had a feeling his neighbor would be drawing an analogy. Reminding him that it was time he freed himself from the restraints of his past that kept love from taking root. That it was time to lift his face to the sun and let romance bloom again.

Although the older man had been on him about that for months, Christopher had always dismissed the suggestion. But lately he'd found himself more open to it. Thanks to Marci.

As if on cue, she appeared from around the far side of Henry's cottage. Taken aback, Christopher watched as she headed for the coiled hose behind the house and turned on the water. Only when she swung around toward the garden, nozzle in hand, did she notice him on the other side of the fence and send him a guarded smile.

"Hi."

"Hi, yourself." His smile was warm and open. "I thought you were done here."

"I was. But I inadvertently uprooted a few plants the other day when I was weeding the last patch, and I thought they might need a drink."

"You drove all the way out here for that?"

She shrugged and moved toward the back of the garden, pulling the hose behind her. "After all my hard work, I don't want any casualties." She adjusted the nozzle to a soft spray and sprinkled a patch of slightly wilted flowers. "Actually, I'm glad I ran into you. I just visited Henry again. You were right earlier today. He's pretty down. Even the chocolate tarts I brought him didn't help a whole lot."

His smile faded. "Yeah, I know. I stopped in after office hours. I tried to convince him his fever is nothing more than a little detour, but I don't think I got through. I'm not sure what to try next. A positive attitude would go a long way toward helping him recover."

"I agree. And I had an idea I wanted to bounce off of you. It's a little ambitious, though."

"So was the elder-assistance plan, but you managed to pull that off. I just read it. You did a stellar job. And I love the name. Caring Connections."

She lifted one shoulder, dismissing her efforts. "Thanks. But all it needed was some legwork to flesh it out."

The slight flush on her cheeks told him the compliment pleased her, despite her offhanded response. Had praise always been in such short supply in her life?

"Nope. Don't buy it. You took a bunch of stream-of-consciousness ideas and molded them into a cohesive, workable plan. And you went out and drummed up support for it. That required talent. And a massive amount of work. So I suspect whatever idea you've come up with to boost Henry's spirits is manageable. Tell me about it."

"Well, when we first met, Henry told me about the gazebo that used to be over there." She gestured to the bare spot in the corner, rimmed by hydrangea bushes about to burst into bloom. "He said he'd built it for his wife years ago, but it had been destroyed in a storm. I got the impression it meant a lot to him."

"It did. It was his wife's favorite place. I was with him the night the storm ripped it apart. He told me that was the only spot where he could still feel her presence."

"I sensed it might be something like that. So my idea is to rebuild it. I saw a picture of it in Henry's kitchen, and the design doesn't look too complicated. Chester's really handy, and I bet I could get him to draw up some plans. I'm sure he'd also help with the construction. And I know I could convince J.C. to pitch in, too."

She moved back to the faucet and turned off the

water, recoiling the hose as she continued to speak. "With Henry scheduled to come home next week, we don't have a lot of time, but I think we could pull this off. After all, they used to build barns in one day years ago. And we could start dropping hints to get him excited about the surprise." She straightened up and regarded him across the yard. "What do you think?"

As Christopher envisioned the gazebo that could fill the empty space in the lawn—and in the older man's heart—a slow smile tugged his lips up. "I think it's brilliant. Henry will love it."

She edged closer, until only a few feet separated them. Close enough for him to see the excitement and pleasure sparking in her eyes. Tempered, however, by a bit of doubt. "It won't be cheap, though."

"Don't worry about the expense. I owe Henry for all the things he's done for me since I arrived. Put me down for the building crew, too. I'm not the world's best carpenter, but if someone points me to a nail I can drive it in."

"Can you imagine his face when we bring him home and he sees it?"

Her enthusiasm was contagious. "It will be quite a moment. I have a key to Henry's house. Do you want to take the picture with you so Chester can look it over?"

"Yes, thanks. That would be great."

"Give me a sec." He strode toward his cottage, retrieved the key and joined her at Henry's back door. After unlocking the door, he removed the photo from the wall while she waited on Henry's porch.

As he handed it over and relocked the door, she examined the image. "I would have liked to meet Marjorie."

At her soft comment, Christopher pocketed the key and looked at the picture over her shoulder. "Me, too. But I know a lot about her from Henry. They shared an amazing love."

"Yeah." She held the picture reverently, her head bowed as she studied it. "That kind doesn't come along very often."

"I've seen examples of it. Every now and then." His words came out husky, and when she gazed up at him, the look in her eyes drove the breath from his lungs.

His first impulse was to kiss her. But he knew she wasn't ready for that.

Without breaking eye contact, he took her shoulders in a gentle grip, turned her toward him and pulled her close. But he didn't claim her lips. He just held her in the shelter of his arms, the photo of Henry's gazebo—a symbol of enduring love— captured between them.

He could feel her trembling, but she didn't pull away as he'd feared she might. And as the seconds ticked by, the silence broken only by the distant crash of the surf, he slowly felt the tension melt from her body. Stroking her back, he nestled her closer, resting his cheek against her curls, marveling at how right she felt in his arms.

Christopher had no idea how long they stood there in the quiet of Henry's garden. But at last she drew a shuddering breath and eased back. Although he missed her warmth at once, he let her go. For now.

Her eyes downcast, she fingered the photo and spoke in a tone that tried a little too hard to sound light and casual. "Henry's picture seems to have cast quite a spell. Pretty soon it'll have us believing in fairy tales."

Putting a finger under her chin, Christopher tipped her head up and locked gazes with her. "The picture isn't the only thing casting a spell. And not all romance is confined to fairy tales."

Tears welled in her eyes—along with an emotion he could only classify as regret. "It is for me."

Before he could process that comment, she backed down the porch steps. "I need t-to go. I'll let you know what Chester says about the gazebo."

With that, she took off at a half run around the side of the cottage.

"Marci, wait…" He started after her, but the panicked look she threw over her shoulder when he reached the arbor told him she needed space. Desperately.

So he remained under the cascade of roses, gripping the top of the gate while she slid into her car and sped away with a crunch of gravel.

He remained that way long after she'd disappeared, staring after her. But at last he pried his fingers off the gate, took a deep breath and shoved his hands into his pockets. Retracing his steps, he paused to look at the spot that had once held the gazebo built with loving care by Henry for a woman whose love continued to enrich his life.

That was what he wanted, Christopher realized. The kind of love shared by Henry and Marjorie— and by his own parents. Yes, he'd made an error in judgment once, mistaking neediness for love. And a deep-seated wariness was a lasting souvenir of the tragic consequences of that relationship.

But Marci wasn't Denise. He'd learned enough about her to feel confident of that.

Yet Marci had her own issues. Her comment tonight about fairy tales reinforced that. As did her hasty exit when things started to get romantic. And they might be just as scary as Denise's. He needed to find out what they were—but unfortunately, he was running out of time. In a little more than two weeks, she would board a plane for Chicago.

And somehow he knew that if he let her walk away, the brightness she'd added to his days would fade away as quickly as clouds could snuff out the Nantucket sun.

Chapter Eleven

"I can't believe how fast this came together."

At Marci's comment, Christopher took a long swig of lemonade and eyed the gazebo that had risen in Henry's backyard in the course of one Sunday afternoon, a mere three days after she'd broached the idea. "Me, neither. Another half hour ought to wrap it up. We couldn't have done it without Chester, though."

They both looked toward the older man in overalls who was perched on a ladder securing a decorative piece of lattice while J.C. held it in place and Edith directed the process from ground level.

"When I gave him the photo, he rubbed his hands together, got this gleam in his eye and said, 'I love projects.' Edith warned me he tended to be slow— she said it took him more than two years to restore the cottage I'm staying in—but she must have lit a fire under him. He came out here Friday afternoon, drew the plans up that night and bought all the material yesterday. It's amazing. And I think our little scheme is working. When I dropped a few hints to Henry about a surprise, I could tell his interest was piqued."

Excitement had put a becoming flush on her cheeks, and her eyes were shining. She'd done a good job evading him since they'd exchanged the hug on Henry's porch, and Christopher couldn't believe how much he'd missed her.

"It is. He's been trying to finagle information out of me every time I visit."

"More to the right, Chester," Edith called. "The lattice is sticking out on the other side over the opening."

"She'd make a good foreman." Christopher grinned and walked a few feet away to pick up another piece of trim. "You want to help me put this up?"

"Sure."

He set his disposable cup aside and moved back to the gazebo. Positioning a ladder beside the opening next to Chester, he took the lattice from Marci.

"I'm sorry to run out on you, but we have plans for tonight." Edith steadied the adjacent ladder as her husband descended. "You and Marci can handle the last two pieces of trim, can't you?"

"We don't have to rush, Edith," the older man protested.

"Chester." She elbowed him. "We have to leave. *Now.*"

Squinting at her, he took off his baseball cap and scratched his head, leaving his unruly cowlick in disarray. "I guess we do."

She gave a satisfied nod and turned to J.C., pinning him with a pointed stare. "J.C., didn't Heather ask you to be back by seven? You could hitch a ride home with us and leave the car for Marci to use later."

He looked from his neighbor to his sister, a grin twitching his lips. "Sounds good to me."

Propping one shoulder against the gazebo, Christopher watched in amusement, admiring Edith's masterful maneuvering.

But it was clear from Marci's narrowed-eyed, mutinous expression that she didn't share his reaction. "None of you said anything earlier about having to leave at a certain time."

"I assumed we'd be done by now. But that's what happens when you have an amateur crew." Edith began to bustle about, collecting some of the scraps of wood while Chester and J.C. broke down the portable sawhorses and headed for Chester's truck with various tools. "You want us to leave one of the ladders, Christopher?"

"If you don't mind. I can use Henry's, but it would

help if Marci had one, too, so she can balance the trim in place while I attach it."

"No problem. Chester gets out this way at least once a week. He'll pick it up on his next trip." Edith planted her hands on her ample hips and surveyed the gazebo. "Looks mighty fine. I imagine Henry will be pleased."

Throughout this exchange, Marci had remained quiet. Her arms were folded tightly across her chest, and she was frowning.

Not good.

"If you want to leave with your brother, it's okay," Christopher said, lowering his voice for her ears only.

She looked at him, clearly torn. "Can you finish this alone?"

"It would be easier with another pair of hands. Besides, I have some things I wanted to discuss with you about Caring Connections."

She shot the cleanup trio another glance. "Look, in case you haven't realized it yet, Edith has a penchant for matchmaking."

His lips quirked into a smile. "Yeah. I figured that out."

"The thing is, I don't want to encourage her. Or my brother. It makes no sense for a lot of reasons. Not the least of which is my imminent departure."

"I'd like to talk to you about that, too."

Before she could respond, Edith called out to them. "We're off. Be sure to get that trim on straight, Christopher."

"I will. Thanks for all your help. You, too, Chester, J.C."

There were a flurry of goodbyes, followed by the cough of a truck engine as it turned over and the crunch of tires on oyster shells. Then silence descended, save for the rhythmic pounding of the surf.

Based on Marci's silence, Christopher assumed she was still processing his last comment. He hadn't planned to bring up the subject of her departure today. But in light of the way she'd been avoiding him, it might be his best opportunity to put out some feelers about her interest in the director job.

And in him.

Snagging a piece of trim, he climbed the ladder. "Let's finish this up before we lose the good light."

Without a word, Marci ascended the other ladder, grasped the trim and held it in place while Christopher secured it.

For the next fifteen minutes, their communication was confined to simple phrases like "A little more to the right" and "Raise it an inch on your side." She didn't ask him to explain his comment; he didn't offer to.

After the last screw was firmly seated in the wood, Christopher put Henry's ladder in the toolshed and leaned Chester's against the railing of the back porch. Then he joined Marci, who had moved off to examine the gazebo from across the yard.

The step-up structure was simple in design, the only ornamentation the lattice panels above each opening and a picketed railing. Constructed of natural wood, it had the raw look of fresh-cut lumber. But Christopher knew it wouldn't take long for the gazebo to acquire the driftwood-colored patina of its predecessor. Large enough to accommodate a café table or a pair of wicker rocking chairs, it would be a perfect place for Henry to recuperate—and remember.

"I can picture Henry sitting there with a mug of coffee in his hand, can't you?"

He smiled. "You must be reading my mind."

"What's your best guess on when he might come home?"

"He didn't have a fever this morning when I stopped by. That's a good sign. If he continues to progress, I'd say he could be back here by Thursday."

"Good. That will give me a chance to make sure all the help I lined up is working out okay before I leave."

He gestured toward the gazebo. "How about we sit for a minute? Might as well enjoy the fruits of our labors."

After a brief hesitation, she acquiesced with a dip of her head. "Okay."

Crossing the lawn, she sat on the elevated floor at the entrance, as close as possible to the upright post on one side.

He joined her in the ample space she'd left for him. Stretching out his legs, he crossed his ankles and leaned back on his palms. The lush green grass and colorful, well-tended flower beds inside the white picket fence provided a striking contrast to the golden sand and sparkling sea beyond.

"Henry has a nice spot here."

Marci gazed out over the water, her expression pensive. "Too bad Patricia can't appreciate that. And how much it means to Henry." She clasped her hands around one knee and looked over at him. "You know, after visiting him at that assisted-living facility, I can't imagine anyone wanting to end their days in a place like that. I'm glad your plan will give older folks another option."

"At this point, it's your plan as much as it is mine."

She shook her head. "No, it was your idea. But I'm glad I could help give it life."

Christopher's heart began to hammer, and he took the plunge. "I'd like for you to do more than that."

She gave him a wary look. "What do you mean?"

"You saw my note about the program deserving a full-time director?"

"Yes."

"With your social-work degree, organizational

skills and empathy for the elderly, you'd be perfect for the job."

Several beats of silence ticked by. "You mean until you find a permanent director?"

"No. I think you'd be a good permanent director."

"I'd have to move here."

"I know. And I can appreciate what that means. You'd have to disrupt your whole life in Chicago. Leave behind everything you know. But you'll be looking for a job anyway. And your brother lives here now, so it wouldn't be as if—"

His phone began to vibrate, and he stifled a groan. Talk about bad timing. He supposed he could ignore it, but his years of medical training had hardwired him to respond to every call.

Pulling the phone off his belt, he checked the caller ID. "It's my exchange. I need to take this."

"No problem."

He pressed the Talk button. "Christopher Morgan. Hold a moment, please." Tapping Mute, he rose. "I'll tell you what. Why don't we grab some sandwiches in town and talk about this? It's past dinnertime. Think about it while I take care of this call, okay?"

Without waiting for her to respond, he moved across the yard. Giving her the opportunity to think up an excuse to cut their evening short. Or refuse the job outright.

But he hoped she wouldn't do that. Because if she

did, she'd be nixing their relationship before it even had a chance to take root.

And that was a possibility he wasn't willing to consider.

From her perch at the edge of Henry's gazebo, Marci sent a silent prayer of thanks heavenward for the interruption. She needed a few minutes to think.

Putting personal feelings aside, the job did appeal to her. As she'd discovered over the past few weeks, she did have an affinity for older folks. Helping people like Henry retain their independence would be satisfying, rewarding work.

As for Christopher's comment about giving up her life in Chicago, that would be no sacrifice. She had few fond memories of the Windy City.

But even if she took the job, even if they found a way to bridge the differences between them, she had very little confidence he'd be able to overlook the past she hadn't yet shared with him. And before she agreed to stay, they'd have to clear that hurdle.

There was no way was she ready to discuss that tonight, however.

Ending the call, Christopher rejoined her. "So how about some dinner? The 'Sconset Café has great sandwiches. We could grab a couple and enjoy them on the beach while we talk."

"I need some time to think about your suggestion, Christopher."

"Okay." He grinned. "But you also have to eat. At least join me for a bite. We deserve it after all our hard work this afternoon. And I promise not to push about the job. Tonight, anyway."

She hesitated. Dinner on the beach with the handsome man smiling down at her sounded wonderful.

"Don't overthink it, Marci. It's just sandwiches."

Giving in to the prodding of her heart, she capitulated. What harm could there be in a casual dinner? "Okay."

"Great. Let me grab a beach towel."

Sixty seconds later, they were strolling down the narrow lane toward the center of the tiny village. Honoring his promise, he didn't bring up the job again. Instead, he kept the conversation light. Once they arrived at the small restaurant, already packed for the evening meal, they worked their way through the crowd and placed their order with the hostess.

"You must be a regular." Marci squeezed through the throng of customers as he ushered her back toward the deck in front.

He grinned. "I'm a typical bachelor, I guess. Cooking isn't my thing. I come here three or four nights a week." He pushed the door open and they stepped outside to wait for their order to be called.

"I can tell. You seem to be on a first-name basis with everyone who works here."

"That's not hard in a town the size of 'Sconset. It doesn't take long to distinguish the year-rounders from the day-trippers and summer people. And ninety-eight percent of the people here fall into the latter two categories." He gestured around at the diners enjoying their meal on the other side of the deck. "I don't recognize any—"

When he stopped abruptly, Marci looked up at him. His complexion had gone pale, and his features had grown taut.

Alarmed, she turned to follow the direction of his gaze. A woman in her late fifties or early sixties, seated at a table for two on the other side of the deck, was staring at him. As Marci watched, she spoke to her gray-haired companion, whose back was to them. He shifted toward them, and the icy look he aimed at Christopher sent a shiver down her spine, despite the balmy weather.

She turned back to him. "What's wrong, Christopher?"

Instead of answering, he took her arm and guided her back inside. Her apprehension escalated at the tremors in his fingers.

"Let's see if our food is ready."

Leaving her inside the door, he strode to the counter and spoke to the hostess. She disappeared into the kitchen, and rather than rejoin her as he waited, Christopher remained where he was. Although Marci couldn't see his face, the tense line of his broad shoulders and his stiff stance communicated distress with a capital D.

What was going on?

A couple of minutes later, the hostess reappeared with two packages wrapped in white paper. She slid them into a large bag, added cans of soda and cellophane-wrapped utensils and handed the bag to Christopher.

When he turned back toward her, the shock had disappeared from his face. But in its place were pain and distress.

As he rejoined her, he spoke before she could voice her concern.

"Let's head for the beach."

Taking her arm, he led her across the elevated wooden platform and down the steps. Christopher never looked back at the two people who'd given him such a venomous perusal. But Marci glanced toward the deck as they passed. They were still watching Christopher, and she had no problem reading the emotion in their eyes.

Hate.

Why in the world would anyone hate such a kind, caring, decent man?

Christopher didn't offer any explanation. Nor did he speak again until they reached the sand.

"How about we go down that way and avoid some of the crowd?" He gestured toward the right, where the deserted beach stretched as far as the eye could see.

"Sure."

They trudged through the deep sand in silence. After about fifty yards he stopped, unrolled the towel he'd tucked under his arm and spread it out. They both sat, and he retrieved the sodas from the bag. But when he tried to open one of the cans, his fingers were shaking so badly she leaned over and took it from him.

"Let me."

Popping the tab, she handed it back and opened the other for herself.

He started to reach into the bag for their sandwiches, but she laid a hand on his arm. "Let's sit for a few minutes, okay? I have a feeling you're not in the mood to eat just now."

In truth, neither was she. She'd never seen Christopher rattled before, and it unnerved her.

As if reading her mind, he took a long swallow of his soda and looked over at her. "Sorry about that. I never expected to see those people again. It was a bit of a jolt."

"I could tell." She ran a finger around the rim of her can, feeling her way. The last thing she wanted to do was butt into Christopher's private business. She had secrets of her own, and she didn't like people pushing her about them, either. "Do you want to tell me who they are?"

He took a deep breath and turned his head toward the sea. The shadows were deepening as the day wound down, robbing the blue water of its sparkle.

"They were part of a very dark chapter in my life. The chapter that led me to Nantucket."

She sifted some sand through her fingers. "I've been curious since we met about your reasons for coming." She chose her words with care, like a soldier crossing a minefield. "I tried asking Henry a few discreet questions, but the most I ever got out of him was that you needed a change. I suspected there was more to the story."

"There is. But I hadn't planned to get into it tonight." He raked his fingers through his hair and shook his head. "There has to be a reason for God's timing on this, though. There always is."

She remained silent, giving him a chance to decide if he wanted to open his heart and share his story with her. She hoped he would. Because if he could find the courage to take her into his confidence about his past, maybe, just maybe, she could do the same.

"It's not what I'd call dinner conversation." He studied her again. "And it's not pretty."

"We can put off dinner for a little while." She returned his searching look steadily.

"Okay." He set his soda in the sand beside him. Pulling up his legs, he rested his forearms on his knees and clasped his hands. Once more he fixed his attention on the horizon.

"Those people are the parents of a woman I dated in Boston. Her name was Denise. I met her at a charity event when she lost her footing going down a step and sprained her ankle. I took a look at it and suggested she have it X-rayed, just to be safe. She was there with a girlfriend who offered to drive her to the E.R., so I helped her out to the car and wished her well."

He closed his eyes, and she watched his Adam's apple bob. "Have you ever had a moment in your life that, in hindsight, you knew was a turning point? One where, if you could relive it, you'd make a different decision?"

Clasping her hands into a tight ball in her lap, Marci confined her answer to a single word. "Yes."

"That's what that night was like for me. If I had it to do over again, I would never have come forward to help."

"That would be out of character for you."

"Maybe. But my life after that would have been a lot less traumatic. And I wouldn't be so cautious around women in distress. Or freaked out by tears."

Marci frowned. "I've gotten teary-eyed around you, and I haven't noticed you freaking out."

"I did the first night, when I saw you crying in the restaurant. But after our paths began to cross, I sensed that tears aren't your standard operating procedure."

"They were with Denise?"

"Not at first." He picked up his soda and took a long drink. "She was grateful for my help at the party, and the next day a huge cookie bouquet arrived at my office. I thought it was overkill, but sweet. Two days later she called and invited me to a symphony concert. She seemed nice enough, and since I love classical music, I accepted. We had a good time, and I reciprocated with an invitation to a movie."

His fingers flexed on the soda can, denting the side, and he set it back on the sand.

"We went out quite a bit over the next month. But she became very possessive. She started calling me three or four times a day, and I began to feel smothered. I also began to pick up some weird vibes. So one night at dinner I told her I thought we needed to cool things off a little and move more slowly.

"I couldn't believe what happened next. She went to pieces right there in the restaurant. Started crying, pleading with me not to reject her, saying she'd do anything as long as I promised to keep seeing her. She was creating such a scene that we left before they even served our entrées. I tried to reason with her in the car on the way home, but I couldn't get through. That's when I realized she had some serious psychological issues."

When he fell silent, Marci was tempted to take his hand. But his rigid posture put her off. It was as if he'd withdrawn into himself, was reaching deep into a dark place in his soul.

"After that night, I knew there was no future in

the relationship. But she wouldn't accept that. Then things got even worse. The phone calls increased, and she'd leave hysterical messages on my answering machine. She began sending me expensive gifts. And when I stopped responding, she started showing up at my condo. Just hanging around, waiting for me to come home from work."

Marci stared at his tense profile. "That's scary."

"Tell me about it. I had no idea how to cope with her. I finally told her I was going to call the police unless she left me alone."

"What happened then?"

He stared at the darkening sea. "She threatened to commit suicide if I cut her off."

Marci drew in a sharp breath. "That's emotional blackmail."

"Yeah." He wiped a hand down his face. "I'd met her parents. We'd had brunch at their house once. So I called to express my concern. They laid into me, too, accusing me of leading her on. And they refused to acknowledge she had any problems." He shook his head. "It was a mess."

The lines in Christopher's face, highlighted by the lengthening shadows cast by the setting sun, told Marci that "mess" didn't begin to capture his obvious anguish and pain.

"Did you see her again?"

"Once. I met her at the Public Garden on my lunch hour one day. She worked near there as a receptionist at a real-estate office her father owned. I only did it because she sounded desperate, and I hoped I could convince her to seek professional help. But it was a mistake. She had another meltdown."

He picked up his can of soda, took another long drink, then crushed the fragile aluminum in his hand.

"The next day she took her life by swallowing a very lethal combination of pills."

The words hung in the air between them as Marci's stomach twisted into a hard knot.

"Oh, Christopher!" Her words came out hushed. "I'm so sorry."

"So was I." His voice roughened, and he cleared his throat. "The guilt was crushing. I felt as if it were my fault, that there must have been something I could have done."

"What?"

He shook his head. "I'm not sure. But her parents certainly thought I was to blame, based on the letter they sent me. She was their only child."

"Why couldn't they see she needed help?"

"I don't know. Maybe it's easier to pretend a problem doesn't exist than to address it in a responsible way."

Marci couldn't argue with that. She'd been there. With the same tragic results.

When she didn't respond, Christopher turned to

her, apology in his eyes. "This was more than you wanted to know, wasn't it?"

"No." She forced her own regrets aside to focus on him. "I'm honored you shared it with me. And I'm sorry for all the pain it's caused you. I take it that's what prompted you to give up your practice and move here?"

"Yes. I started over. And continued to struggle with the guilt."

"It wasn't your fault, Christopher."

"I've finally accepted that. But it *has* made me question my judgment about women."

"I can understand that."

"I get good vibes from you, though."

At the sudden tenderness in his tone, she felt the pressure of tears in her throat and fumbled for her own soda, buying herself a moment to rein in her emotions. She didn't have Denise's psychological issues, but she did have secrets. And in the end, they could be just as big a turnoff for Christopher as the problems of his Boston girlfriend.

Taking a swig, she resettled the can in the sand and summoned up a smile. "Well, I don't know about vibes, but I do know we'll be eating in the dark if we don't start our sandwiches. Are you in the mood for dinner, or should we call it a night?"

"I can eat. To be honest, it felt good to talk about the whole thing. The only other person here who's heard my story is Henry." He reached into the bag and withdrew the sandwiches. Handing hers over, he began to unwrap his.

"What did he have to say about it?" Marci peeled back the paper on her sandwich, her own appetite nonexistent.

The whisper of a smile played at his lips. "That what happened with Denise wasn't my fault. That the problem was hers, not mine. Henry is very loyal."

"And right."

"It took me a long time to accept that. But thanks to a lot of prayer and a lot of reflection, I'm finally coming around." He took a bite of his sandwich.

Marci followed his lead, forcing herself to chew and swallow.

"I think we've covered enough heavy stuff for one night. Why don't we talk about Henry's coming-home party?" he suggested.

"Sounds good to me."

For the rest of their meal, they focused on the older man. And by the time they walked back down the oyster-shell lane toward his cottage, Marci felt more relaxed. She could tell he did, too.

Pausing beside her car, she dug through her purse for the key as he opened the door for her. "Thanks for dinner."

"It was my pleasure."

He leaned against the hood and folded his arms over his chest, obviously in no hurry to end the evening. A full moon overhead gave an ethereal glow to the landscape, and she could glimpse the shimmering sea between Henry's cottage and the one Christopher occupied.

She couldn't imagine a more romantic scene.

Stifling that thought, she tossed her purse onto the passenger seat and pasted on a smile as she looked at him over the door. "Thanks again."

He pushed off from the hood and moved closer.

Too close.

"I have something I want to ask you. Not related to the job."

She gripped the edge of the door with one hand, trying to ignore the powerful magnetism that was sending her heart into a tailspin as he circled around to stand in front of her.

"Okay."

"My parents are coming to Nantucket for a couple of days this week. We're planning to go to dinner on Tuesday. I'd be honored if you'd join us."

He was inviting her to meet his parents.

"I…uh…wouldn't want them to get the wrong idea. If you know what I mean."

"I know what you mean." He closed the distance between them. "And I think they'll get exactly the right idea." Slowly he reached up and touched her cheek.

Her breath caught in her throat.

"We've been dancing around the attraction

between us since the beginning, Marci. I think we need to explore it. Don't you?"

She might—if she could get her mind in gear. But with Christopher a whisper away, the gentle brush of his fingertips warming her cheek and the moon silvering the world around her, she couldn't seem to engage the left side of her brain.

He smiled down at her. "I don't think I've ever rendered a woman speechless before. But I do agree that talk is superfluous."

Resting one hand lightly on her shoulder, he captured one of her springy curls in his strong, lean fingers. Then, his eyes darkening, he kissed her.

Marci stopped breathing.

It had been years since she'd been kissed. And never like this. With tenderness. And reverence. And deep caring.

She wanted it to go on forever.

Instead, Christopher backed off, leaving her still clinging to the door—and to his shirt. She'd bunched the front into her fist, she realized, releasing a handful of wrinkles.

"Did I convince you?"

His voice sounded several shades deeper than usual. And oh-so-appealing. It took every ounce of her willpower not to throw herself back into his arms.

"Yeah." It was the only possible response.

The smile he gave her warmed her all the way to her toes. "I'll call you with the details."

He lifted a hand once more to her hair, as if savoring the feel of it between his fingers. Then, with a sigh, he backed off. "Drive safe."

She nodded, still not trusting her voice.

It took her two tries to get the key into the ignition. And as she pulled away, her gaze flitted between the road and her rearview mirror, where the tall, broad-shouldered man bathed in moonlight was reflected.

He looked like a figure from a dream. The sort of perfect man a lonely woman might conjure up in her imagination to fill the empty place in her heart.

Except Christopher Morgan was real.

But when moonlight and dreams gave way to reality and the harsh light of day, would he continue to hang around—or would he vanish like the mist of a Nantucket morning?

Chapter Twelve

"I'm perfectly capable of doing that myself, thank you."

As Henry shooed away the aide who was trying to help him put on his robe, Marci grinned from the doorway. Each time she'd visited the assisted-living facility in the past few days, he'd been livelier.

Spotting her, he grinned back. "Well, now, if that isn't a sight for sore eyes."

"If you need me, ring the bell, Mr. Calhoun," the young aide said.

"I'll do that. But I expect I'll be fine. Especially now that I have such a pretty visitor."

As the woman exited, Marci strolled over to Henry. "You're looking good."

"I'm feeling better. And getting awful tired of this place."

"Christopher says he expects to spring you on

Thursday. Just in time for Independence Day. How appropriate is that?"

"Couldn't be better." He motioned her to a chair near the window and took the facing one. "He was in this morning. Mentioned you were having dinner with him and his parents tonight."

She shifted in her seat, surprised Christopher had passed on that bit of news. "He caught me at a weak moment."

He squinted at her. "Don't you like him?"

"Sure. What's not to like?" She tried for a flippant tone. "But I don't want to give his parents the wrong impression."

"What impression would that be?"

"You know…that there's something going on between us."

Henry leaned back and chuckled. "'There are none so blind as those that will not see,' to quote an Irish fellow from hundreds of years ago. Still true today, too."

Marci narrowed her eyes. "What's that supposed to mean?"

"I may be old, but there's nothing wrong with my powers of perception. Anyone in the same room with you two would have to be dead not to pick up the chemistry."

With a sigh of capitulation, Marci slumped back in her chair. "Okay. Maybe there's a spark."

"A spark." Henry hooted with laughter. "My dear girl, it's like Fourth of July."

She made a face. "Very funny. That still doesn't mean there's anything going on."

"There *should* be."

She gave him an exasperated look. "Why are you so interested, anyway?"

"Because I've been after that boy for two years to find himself a woman to romance. Not just any woman, mind you. Someone good and kind and smart and funny and spunky. I knew the minute I laid eyes on you that you were his perfect match."

Marci wanted to sink through the floor. First, because her feelings had been so transparent. And second, because no way would she ever be worthy of a man like Christopher—no matter how much J.C. tried to build up her self-esteem. Her one slim hope was that if Christopher's interest in her was *really* serious—and that was a big if, no matter what Henry thought—he might find a way to overlook her past.

And if a man with such a kind and generous heart couldn't manage that, she was sunk. Forever.

Shoving that depressing thought aside, she wagged a warning finger at the older man. "Don't read too much into this thing with Christopher's parents, Henry. It's just a dinner. We've never even been out on a date."

"I bet he's kissed you, though."

Try as she might, she couldn't stop the sudden rush of warmth that flooded her cheeks.

"Hot dog!" Henry slapped his hand against his thigh in glee. "I'm proud of that boy. I always knew he had good judgment, and this proves it." He cocked his head. "I'm guessing he told you about Denise."

"Yes. And it's also clear he wants to be cautious." She paused and glanced out the window. "The truth is, I may not be the best woman for him, Henry. There are a lot of reasons why it might not work."

"Name one."

"We come from very different worlds in terms of family life, finances, exposure to culture."

"Name an important one."

"That *is* important."

"No, it's not. If Marjorie and I could find a way to make it work, you can, too."

"What do you mean?"

"Marjorie and I met at a USO dance. Prettiest little thing I'd ever seen. Plus a first-class brain. My kind of woman. We felt the spark right away, too.

"Trouble was, her father was a self-made man with a fifth-grade education who didn't much value formal education. He'd risen to the top in his field and made a lot of money after learning everything he needed to know in the school of hard knocks. By his standards, he was successful. He'd built a flour-ishing company, had a nice house in a nice neighborhood, didn't want for any material possession. And he was determined that the man who married his daughter would measure up to that yardstick as well."

With a rueful twist of his lips, Henry shook his head. "That sure wasn't me. My idea of success was opening the minds of young people to the works of Shakespeare, or helping them learn to appreciate and love the masterful use of language."

When he stopped, Marci leaned forward, intrigued. "How did you reconcile that difference?"

"We didn't. But that didn't stop Marjorie from loving me. She said she didn't care about all the trappings of wealth. That none of that mattered if she couldn't have the man she loved. So she left it all behind. And I don't think she ever regretted it, not for one second. We had a wonderful life together here on Nantucket."

Marci gave him a wistful smile. "That's a beautiful story, Henry."

"True, too. And if it worked out for me, it can work out for you."

If the only stumbling block with Christopher was their different backgrounds, Henry might be right, Marci conceded as she took in the flawless blue sky outside the window. Christopher didn't strike her as the type of man who would let differences in class or financial status dictate his circle of acquaintances. Or choice of wife.

But there was much more they'd have to overcome.

"You don't look convinced."

At the older man's comment, she turned back to him.

"I'm supposed to be leaving in less than two weeks, Henry."

"Christopher told me he offered you the director job for Caring Connections."

She played with the zipper on her purse. "I haven't decided what to do about that."

"You want my opinion? Take it. You can always go back to Chicago if things don't work out. One lesson I've learned in life is never pass up an opportunity. Some of them only come around once." He let a few beats of silence pass, then leaned forward with an impish grin. "Now give me another hint about this surprise you and Christopher have cooked up for me at home."

Forcing herself to switch gears, Marci bantered back and forth with the older man, evading his questions about the surprise while dropping a few more tantalizing hints.

Half an hour later, when Henry pushed her out the door to go get ready for her date—as he insisted on calling it—Marci didn't argue. She did want to look her best tonight.

Because even though she had serious doubts about the future for her and Christopher, Henry was right. Some opportunities only came around once.

And given the strong connection between them, she'd be a fool not to give this thing a chance.

As Christopher ascended the steps to the porch of The Summer House restaurant, high on a bluff on the outskirts of 'Sconset, he tapped in the number his exchange had passed on. While the call went through, he took in the sweeping view of the Atlantic. In a way he was glad his father had been delayed at the hotel with a business call. Using the excuse that he didn't want to keep Marci waiting, he'd gone on ahead. If he was lucky, he might have a few minutes with her before his parents showed up.

Other than a quick phone call finalizing tonight's arrangements, he hadn't seen her since their parting Sunday night. Nor had that brief conversation given him a reading on her feelings.

Kissing her had been risky. But the magic of the moonlight had chased away common sense. And since she hadn't exactly jumped at the chance to take the director job, he'd hoped the kiss might help seal the deal.

It hadn't. And when he'd broached the subject on the phone yesterday, she'd sidestepped it.

He tried not to think about the ticking clock.

Or the plane that would whisk her away in eleven days.

As he chatted with his patient on the phone, he turned away from the sea and glanced at the bar through the bank of tall French windows. Scanning the room, he spotted a blonde with fabulous legs in a black cocktail dress.

Marci was already here.

Still talking to his patient, he moved across the porch and stepped inside. Marci was angled away from him in the bar area, and he stayed off to the side to finish the call, his mind only half on the conversation as he leaned one shoulder against the wall. His patient's stuffy nose didn't require total concentration. He'd much rather focus on the lovely woman waiting for him.

Apparently the brawny thirty-something guy at the bar felt the same way, Christopher realized, noting the direction of the man's gaze.

It was aimed at Marci's legs.

The guy picked up his drink, slid off his bar stool and ambled over to Marci. Christopher had no trouble hearing his slightly slurred voice. "Hi gorgeous. Can I buy you a drink?"

Marci turned slightly toward the guy and gave him a quick once-over. "No, thank you. I'm waiting for someone."

"You don't have to wait alone."

The dark-haired jerk leered at her and moved closer. Too close. "No one should let a lovely lady cool her heels."

Ending the call with uncharacteristic abruptness, Christopher strode toward the duo. Marci had no doubt been deflecting passes from men for years. But she wasn't going to have to get rid of *this* guy alone, he resolved, his jaw tightening.

As he joined them, both turned in his direction. Ignoring Marci's surprised look, he took her arm and eased her behind him, then turned to face her "admirer." The guy's eyes were a bit glassy, his reflexes slow, and when he took a startled step back his drink sloshed out of his glass as he struggled to keep his balance. The smell of alcohol on his breath was potent.

Christopher gave him a cold, hard stare. "Back off, mister. The lady isn't interested."

"Hey, buddy, I'm not looking for trouble." The guy took another step back and held up a hand, palm forward.

"Good." Christopher kept his own hand firmly on Marci's arm and urged her away from the bar and around a corner. "Are you okay?"

Her lips tipped into a wry smile that didn't quite reach her eyes. "Sure. Trust me, I've run into that type before."

"I'm sorry you've had to deal with that kind of stuff, Marci. More than I can say. And I'm also sorry about what just happened. This is usually a classy place."

"Hey, it's okay. Jerks are everywhere. I'm used to it. Blonde hair and a decent body seem to attract men the same way light attracts moths."

She spoke in a matter-of-fact tone, with not even the barest hint of conceit. Christopher figured she'd long ago come to consider her good looks as much a curse as a blessing. He could see why, after tonight.

"It's *not* okay." He touched her face, his fingers gently stroking her cheek, and heard her soft intake of breath. "And for the record, I like you for a lot of reasons that go way beyond skin deep."

At his comment, he felt a slight tremor run through her. "Thank you. And thank you for stepping in tonight. No one's ever done that before."

"Maybe that's because you come across as such a strong person. And I mean that as a compliment. I'm sure you were perfectly capable of handling that jerk tonight."

Her green irises had grown soft during their exchange, but now they hardened. "I was. A drink in the face usually does the trick."

He arched an eyebrow. "An effective technique, I imagine."

She gripped her black clutch purse. "Yeah. But it tends to draw attention. I prefer not to make a scene unless it's absolutely necessary." She took a deep breath and leaned sideways to glance toward the entrance. "Are your parents here?"

He checked over his shoulder. "Not yet. Dad got a call from the office that delayed him. They should be along any minute."

"I think I'll visit the ladies' room, then."

"You want me to walk with you?"

A mirthless smile touched her lips. "I appreciate the offer. But I can take care of myself."

Without waiting for a reply, she walked away, passing the lounge area without sparing it a glance.

As she disappeared, Christopher headed toward the foyer to wait for his parents, mulling over her parting comment. He didn't doubt the truth of it. She did know how to take care of herself.

But that didn't stop him from wanting to do it for her.

It had been more than two years since he'd felt the kind of strong protective instinct that had overtaken him tonight. Since he'd *let* himself feel it. After Denise, those kinds of feelings had scared him.

Now they made him feel good.

And that reinforced his decision to push Marci to take the director job—for reasons that had nothing to do with her professional qualifications.

Marci pulled her comb out of her purse and ran it through her hair, willing her churning stomach to settle down. Unless she calmed down, she wouldn't be able to eat a bite of dinner.

Meeting Christopher's parents was nerve-wracking enough. She hadn't needed that little interlude in the bar.

Nor had she needed his admission about his feelings toward her.

That had only reminded her of the pressing need to share her past with him before things got even more serious.

That line of thought however, was *not* going to calm her.

Think about Henry's homecoming, she ordered herself. *And take some slow, deep breaths.*

After a few minutes, when she felt less stressed, she exited the ladies' room and worked her way back to the entrance.

She spotted Christopher before he saw her. In his beige slacks, navy blue sport coat and open-necked white shirt, he looked very preppy. And very handsome.

But it was the two people with him who drew her attention.

A slender woman with reddish-brown hair swept back into a chic chignon stood beside a gray-haired man who fell an inch or two shy of Christopher's height. He, too, wore a sport coat—wheat-colored—with dark slacks and a blue shirt.

As she drew close, Marci saw the family resemblance at once. Christopher had his father's lean build and broad shoulders. From his mother he'd inherited his blue eyes and strong cheekbones.

All at once the older woman turned toward her. Smiling, she touched Christopher's arm.

If his mother's smile had been warm, Christopher's melted her heart. As if sensing her trepidation, he came toward her and took her hand in a firm clasp, weaving his fingers with hers. Giving her a reassuring squeeze, he drew her into the circle of his family and made the introductions.

Marci shook hands with Christopher's father and found herself pulled into a hug with his mother.

"Call us Brad and Carol," the older woman told her. "We're a very low-key, informal bunch."

That might be true, but the understated elegance of her attire reeked of class—and money. Marci couldn't afford expensive outfits herself, but she could spot quality. In people and clothes.

And Christopher's parents had it in spades.

As she and Christopher followed his parents to their table, she smoothed down the skirt of her dress. It was the same black number she'd worn to J.C.'s wedding, bought on sale at Target, and somewhat the worse for wear after her trek through the rain that night.

No way could the polyester frock compare to Carol's silk shantung sheath, which matched the hue of the blue hydrangeas beginning to bloom outside the window. And now that she'd seen Carol's discreet but stunning gold and diamond pendant, she wished she'd left her cheap costume pearls at the cottage.

They were shown to a linen-covered table by the

window that offered a panoramic view of the sea. As Marci took her seat and opened the menu the waiter handed her, she stifled a gasp. A person could eat at Ronnie's for a month on what this dinner for four was going to cost!

"Does that sound good, Marci?"

At Christopher's question, she turned to him. "I'm sorry, I was distracted for a minute."

"I'm having that problem myself." He winked at her, and her heart skipped a beat. "Do you like crab?"

"Sure." Not that she'd ever eaten much of it. It wasn't a menu staple at Ronnie's.

"How about some crab cakes to start?"

"Okay.

"Christopher tells us you've just gotten your master's in social work, Marci. Congratulations," Carol said.

"Thank you."

"And you came to Nantucket for your brother's wedding?"

"Yes."

"What brought him here?"

"He was a detective in Chicago and took a leave of absence." Marci closed the menu and set it aside. "A friend of his is the police chief here, so he took what was supposed to be a temporary job as a summer officer. He ended up meeting his future wife, and the rest is history."

"It's odd how you can meet the right person in the most unexpected places, isn't it?" She cast an amused glance at her son.

Squirming in her seat, Marci diverted the conversation with a question of her own. "How did you two meet?"

Carol smiled at Brad and took his hand. "Shall I tell the story, or do you want to?"

"You do a much better job of it," Brad deferred.

"All right. We were both students at Harvard. Brad was in the law school, and I was in government with my sights set on a diplomatic career in some exotic location. Our paths never crossed on campus, but one summer I did an internship in Paris. Brad happened to be doing a typical student tour of the continent with some of his buddies, and we ran into each other under the Eiffel Tower, of all places. We started chatting, and realized we were both from Harvard. As you said about your brother, the rest is history."

"Mom and Dad just got back from Paris," Christopher offered as he helped himself to a roll. "They celebrated their fortieth anniversary with dinner in the Eiffel Tower."

"And she looked as beautiful as the day I met her," Brad added.

The waiter delivered the appetizers, saving Marci from having to reply. That was providential, since she had no idea how to respond. There was no such thing as a student tour of Europe in her world. Nor had there been trips to Paris. Or a Harvard education.

"Did Mark call you today?" Carol asked Christopher when the waiter departed.

"Yes. The whole crew was on the phone with their usual off-key rendition of 'Happy Birthday.' And Eric—" Christopher turned to Marci "—he's my seven-year-old nephew—wanted to tell me all about the trip to Bermuda."

Marci stared at him. "Is today your birthday?"

"Yes. But I'm trying to ignore them these days." He grinned at her.

"You're too young to use that line," his father admonished. "Wait till you're our age. We've heard all about Bermuda, too. A dozen times."

His brother's family vacationed in Bermuda.

Marci picked at her crab cake, feeling more and more as if she'd stepped into an alternate universe. These people went to Europe—and other foreign places—as matter-of-factly as she went to the Loop.

"Say, Christopher, you'll never guess who we had dinner with the other night. He wanted us to pass on his regards."

He lifted one shoulder in response to his father's comment. "I have no idea."

When the older man mentioned one of the Supreme Court justices, Marci almost choked on the sip of water she'd taken.

"Are you okay?" Christopher gave her a solicitous look and touched her shoulder.

"Fine," she coughed out the word.

"Anyway, he's thinking about retiring. Told me I ought to do the same."

"Maybe you should consider it. That would give you and Mom the chance to spend some time in Italy and take that Greek island cruise you've always talked about."

"I might cut back. But it's hard to step away from a firm with your name on it."

"There are plenty of lawyers there who could pick up the slack," Carol commented.

Christopher's father owned a law firm.

Any hope she'd harbored about meshing their two worlds was dwindling as fast as an ice cube in Ronnie's sweltering kitchen. Christopher had never talked about *any* of this stuff! But she supposed she shouldn't be surprised. He was one of the most unpretentious people she'd ever met.

"Tell us more about your family, Marci."

At Carol's question, a bite of crab cake got caught in her throat.

Coaxing her lips into the semblance of a smile, she took a drink of water and prayed for inspiration. She didn't want to lie, but this wasn't the time to go into her dysfunctional childhood.

"Besides J.C., I have one other brother. He's still in Illinois. But we stay in close touch."

She was saved from further explanation by the waiter's return, and Marci used the food-ordering interlude to think up questions that would deflect the attention from her.

As they all handed over their menus, she addressed Christopher's mother. "I've never been to Paris. I'd love to hear more about your trip."

That conversation took them through their salads and up to the delivery of their entrées.

Poking at her seared halibut, Marci searched for another innocuous topic. She'd already gleaned that Carol didn't have a career outside the home, but she had a feeling the dynamic woman across from her was the type who kept busy with worthwhile causes. A discussion of those should carry them through the entrée portion of the meal.

"So tell me, Carol. Do you have any special interests?"

The older woman laughed. "Too many, to hear Brad talk." She sent her husband an affectionate glance.

"Only because you manage to rope me into all kinds of activities," he teased. "I'll never forget the year you signed us up to serve Thanksgiving dinner at a homeless shelter and we had to traipse all the way downtown on streets better suited to ice hockey than driving."

"Yeah." Christopher chuckled. "Mark and I threw our skates in the car just in case."

"But you know what? That was one of our best

Thanksgivings. All of the people we served were so grateful," Carol said. "And it made us appreciate our blessings all the more."

"That's true," Brad agreed.

"In terms of ongoing activities, though, my volunteer commitment to Birthright means the most to me," Carol said. "I didn't know much about the organization until Christopher joined the board and got me involved. It's such worthwhile work. Can you imagine anything better than saving the lives of unborn children?"

The crab cake congealed in Marci's stomach.

"Anyway, I've been volunteering there one day a week for the past five years. By the way, Christopher, Allison asked me to say hello."

"How's she doing?"

"Great. She's one of the best workers there and has really gotten her act together. Can you believe Sam is almost four?"

Christopher shook his head. "Time slips away, doesn't it? I'm glad things are going well for her."

"Allison was a patient of Christopher's at the clinic," Carol explained to Marci. At the younger woman's blank look, she tipped her head. "He's told you about the clinic, hasn't he?"

"No." Marci was beginning to realize how little she knew about the man beside her.

"Why am I not surprised?" Carol gave Christopher an affectionate smile.

"It's no big deal, Mom."

"It is to the people you treated." She redirected her attention to Marci. "He volunteered at this clinic in a, shall we say, less-than-desirable area of Boston. Allison came in asking about an abortion. She'd had one a couple of years before and found herself back in the same situation. Different father. Christopher encouraged her to at least talk to the people at Birthright.

"Well, long story short, thanks to his efforts, she decided to not only have the baby, but keep it. As you can imagine, since she speaks from personal experience, she's very effective when talking with young women who are thinking about making a different choice."

"We need more women like her," Christopher added. "Think of all the innocent lives we could save if we could help women understand that there are better ways of dealing with an unplanned pregnancy than killing the child."

Marci couldn't think of one thing to say in response.

When the silence lengthened, Christopher stepped in. "Speaking of helping people out, I have some news on the elder-assistance plan I've been working on."

The conversation during the remainder of the meal focused on Caring Connections, but though Christopher played up her role and tried to draw her in, Marci didn't add much. How could she maintain an upbeat front when the fairy-tale dreams she'd allowed herself to indulge in were disintegrating before her eyes?

As dinner wound down, Christopher leaned close to her ear. "Are you okay?"

"Yes. Why?"

"You didn't eat much."

She surveyed her plate. Most of her entrée was untouched.

"Would you like to take that home, miss?"

A waiter was hovering at her shoulder, waiting for her response. At the prices this place charged, she'd feel guilty about wasting her food. But did well-bred people take food home from a classy joint like this?

"You're lucky you live here," Carol said. "I'd take mine home if I wasn't staying in a hotel."

That cinched it.

"Yes, please," Marci told the waiter.

No sooner had he whisked her plate away than another waiter appeared carrying a cake with flickering candles on top. He set it in front of Christopher.

"Shall we sing?" Brad asked.

"No. The wake-up call rendition this morning was sufficient, thanks." Christopher shook his head. "When did you arrange this?"

"Your mother took care of it."

"What's a birthday without a cake?" Carol said. "Make a wish."

Marci had folded her hands tightly in her lap as she regarded the cake, but all at once Christopher reached out and covered them with one of his.

Startled, she lifted her chin to meet his gaze. In his eyes she saw his wish—but also concern. As if he sensed something was amiss.

And there was. She didn't belong here, in this close-knit family circle. Thanks to her own sordid family history and a past she couldn't change.

Although the temptation to simply get up and walk out was strong, she refrained. No way did she want to cause a scene or ruin Christopher's birthday.

But the instant they finished their cake, she was out of here.

Chapter Thirteen

Something was very wrong.

As Christopher ate his last bite of cake, he took a quick look at Marci. She'd eaten no more than a couple forkfuls of her dessert, mashing the remainder into a small, gooey lump in the middle of her plate. And she'd grown increasingly more subdued as the meal had progressed.

He supposed it was possible her encounter with the guy in the bar was responsible for the pall that had fallen over her, but some instinct told him that wasn't the explanation.

Maybe she was just nervous, he reflected, clenching his napkin in his lap. Meeting a guy's parents was a big deal, even though his mom and dad had done their best to put her at ease with their usual charm and grace. But he didn't think that was the reason for her withdrawal, either.

Too bad she'd insisted on driving herself tonight. If she'd let him pick her up, the ride back to the main town would have given him plenty of opportunity to try and ferret out the reasons for her mood shift.

That not being a possibility, he was left with only one alternative.

Beside him, Marci set her napkin on the table and reached for her purse. "It's been lovely meeting you both." She directed her comment to his parents. "I hope you won't mind if I make it an early evening, but I have a busy day tomorrow."

She rose, and Brad immediately did the same. Christopher wasn't far behind.

"Of course not, my dear." Carol smiled and extended her hand. Marci took it, then shook Brad's.

"Drive safe," the older man said.

"I'll walk you to your car."

At Christopher's comment, she turned to him. An emotion that looked a lot like panic flashed across her eyes.

"That's not necessary."

"Yes, it is." He set his own napkin on the table, stepped back and waited for her to precede him. Short of making a scene, he'd left her no option but to go with him. And she'd told him earlier she didn't like scenes.

Still, he'd expected her jaw to tip up just a bit in defiance. But to his surprise, he saw it tremble very subtly instead, and noted an almost imperceptible droop of her shoulders.

With one more stiff smile at his parents, she eased past him and headed for the door, Christopher close on her heels.

Once outside she took off at a good clip. But his stride was longer, and he moved beside her, taking her arm as they walked down the restaurant path toward the quiet lane on the bluff above the beach where she'd parked.

"You want to tell me what's wrong?"

She missed a step, and he tightened his grip. Once she regained her balance, she picked up her pace again. "Nothing's wrong."

"Sorry. Not buying it."

Silence.

"Come on, Marci, talk to me."

As they approached her car, she fumbled through her purse for her key. "Why didn't you tell me it was your birthday?"

Was that what this was all about?

"I didn't want you to feel obligated to get me a present. Your presence at this dinner was gift enough. Is that why you're upset?"

"I'm not upset."

"Marci." He took her upper arms in his hands and forced her to look at him. "I know you're upset. Just tell me what's wrong, okay?"

He could feel her trembling as they stood there

in the moonlight, the faint crash of the sea on the beach below them unable to mask her soft, sad sigh.

"I'm sorry, Christopher, but this thing between us…it's not going to work."

His mouth went dry. "Why not?"

"Our different backgrounds, for one thing. I knew you came from money, but…" She shook her head, as if at a loss for words. "Look, your parents and brother fly to exotic places as easily as I take the bus downtown. Your dad owns a law firm. A Supreme Court justice is a family friend. Trust me, blue-collar Marci would never fit into your blue-blood family."

He should have told her more about his family's circumstances, Christopher realized with a sinking feeling. But it had never occurred to him it would be an issue for her. It wasn't for him.

"You have as much class as anyone I've ever met, Marci. And I don't care about your background. Family pedigree—or lack of one—has nothing to do with how I feel about you."

"I would never fit into your world, Christopher." There was a hint of tears in her words now. "There are probably a dozen socialites waiting for you to come back to Boston. Women who know which fork to use with which course. Who know which side of the Seine is frequented by high-class people. Do yourself a favor. Forget about me and hook up with the right kind of woman."

Stunned, Christopher stared at her. For the first time in their acquaintance she'd given him a revealing glimpse of the insecure woman behind the tough facade she presented to the world. A woman whose trust level with men was as low as the diminutive Brant Point Light, thanks to jerks like the guy in the bar. Whose hardscrabble background made her feel unworthy of mingling with what she considered the upper class.

Somehow he had to convince her that the right kind of woman for him was named Marci Clay.

"Let's talk about this, okay?" He tried to twine his fingers with hers, but she shook his hand off.

"Talking won't change our backgrounds."

"I told you, I don't care about that. And neither do my parents. They're not snobs."

"They also don't know my family history." There was a touch of anguish in her tone now as she looked up at him and the moon turned her too-pale skin to alabaster. "Did you tell them my father deserted us? That we lived in a tenement? That J.C. raised us?"

"No." He raked his fingers through his hair and shoved one hand into the pocket of his slacks. "It never came up."

"It will. And there's a lot more you don't know."

"Such as?"

A few beats of silence ticked by as their gazes locked. When she spoke, the words came out broken, like shells on a beach that have been pounded by the elements. "Your mom asked me about my other brother tonight. I evaded the question. You know why? Nathan's serving time in prison for armed robbery."

Jolted, Christopher took a second to regroup. "Okay. So you have a black sheep in the family. A lot of families do."

"He's not a black sheep anymore. We reconciled last summer, after being estranged for a dozen years. And when he's released next spring, I intend to do whatever I can to help him get a new start. So an ex-con is going to be part of my life. How do you think your parents will react to that?"

"If things become serious between us, they'll be completely supportive."

"How do *you* feel about it?"

"If he's important in your life, he'll be important in mine."

No response.

"Marci, the only thing that matters is the way we feel about each other. I still want you to take the Caring Connections director job."

More silence, while he prayed she wouldn't turn him down outright.

"I'll tell you what." The tense line of her shoulders collapsed, and she suddenly sounded bone weary. "How about we let things rest for a day or two? Once we get Henry home and settled, we can talk again. You might feel differently once all this sinks in."

"That's not going to happen."

"Humor me, okay?"

"I'm not going to change my mind."

"Please, Christopher…don't push on this tonight. Your parents are waiting for you, and I don't want to spoil your birthday."

Without giving him a chance to respond, she slipped into the car and pulled the door shut behind her.

He thought about trying to stop her. To *make* her listen. But it was obvious she wasn't in a receptive mood tonight.

Stepping back, he let her drive away—for now. But he wasn't going to give up without a fight.

Marci adjusted a fork on one of the lace-edged placemats she'd found in Henry's dining room. They'd moved the café table from Edith's guest cottage to the gazebo for the welcome-home dinner, and she'd set it with Henry's good dishes. A tiny vase in the center held an array of flowers from his garden, which she'd weeded once more yesterday. The yard looked pristine.

The dinner was ready, too. She and Heather had prepared the meal together at The Devon Rose earlier today—including the chocolate tarts Henry loved. It was all waiting in his kitchen.

Everything was perfect for his homecoming.

Except the relationship between his two main benefactors.

Marci hadn't seen Christopher since the dinner with his parents two nights ago. Meaning he'd either been very busy or was having second thoughts.

For both their sakes, she hoped it was the latter.

Because if he persisted, she would be forced to tell him her secret. And from what she'd gathered at his birthday dinner, she'd face a rejection far more devastating—and deeply personal—than one based purely on family background.

The crunch of tires interrupted her musing, and she rubbed her palms on her denim skirt. There'd be time to think about her own problems later. For now, she wanted to give Henry her full attention— and the joyous homecoming he deserved.

Moving to the porch, Marci positioned herself for a good view of Henry's face as he came around the back corner of the house and got his first glimpse of the gazebo that had risen in the empty corner he'd left behind.

She heard a car door shut. Then another. Next came the sound of the latch on the gate being lifted. Her heart began to thud.

Fifteen seconds later, Henry rounded the corner.

And came to a dead stop.

From her spot half shielded by a profuse hydrangea bush, Marci watched his face.

First came shock. Then awe. Then delight, followed by a flush of pleasure that pinkened his cheeks.

"My." She heard his hushed comment, saw the sudden sheen in his eyes, and looked at Christopher. He was standing on the other side of the older man, and their gazes met over Henry's head. For a brief instant, the walls between them dissolved and their hearts touched in a moment of shared joy and satisfaction.

Together, they'd brought Henry home again.

And thanks to Caring Connections, they'd be doing the same for many more people in the future.

Stepping down from the porch, Marci crossed the lawn to join them.

"Did we get it right, Henry?"

He turned to her, his eyes still misty. "The only thing missing is Marjorie. But you know what? I can feel her presence again for the first time in two years." He surveyed the yard and shook his head in wonder. "The garden is just like she always kept it, and the gazebo is perfect. How did you manage this?"

"We showed Chester Shaw the photo by your kitchen table, and he drew up the plans. He and Christopher and my brother pitched in to build it."

"But it was all Marci's idea," Christopher added.

Henry smiled at her. "You are one special lady, Marci Clay. Would you mind if an old man gave you a hug?"

"Well, I don't see any old men around here. But I'd love to have a hug from you."

She stepped into his thin arms, and he gave her a good squeeze. Shifting toward Christopher, he stuck out his hand. "Thank you both. For everything."

"Hey, the evening's just getting started," Marci said. "You two gentlemen take your seats and I'll rustle up the first course."

By the time she returned with a tray of salads, Henry was settled into his place at the table.

"You know, I wasn't real sure I'd ever be looking at this view again," he admitted as she put his salad in front of him.

"I told you all along you'd come home." Marci set the tray aside and took her place.

"I guess the good Lord was watching out for me. I think a little prayer of thanks is in order."

Without waiting for a response, he bowed his head. Christopher did likewise. Marci wasn't accustomed to praying before meals, but if ever there was a day to be thankful, this was it. And even though she wasn't into formal prayers, she'd been sending a few heavenward since her visit to church with Christopher. That hour in the Lord's house had given her an unexpected sense of peace—and an inkling about the reason for J.C.'s staunch faith and Nathan's conversion.

"Lord, we thank You for this day of great blessings. For this meal shared with friends. For eyes to see and ears to hear the beauty of Your sea and sky and flowers. For restored health and hope for tomorrow.

"I thank You, too, for sending these two special people into my life when I needed them most. Please bless them as You blessed me, with the kind of love that transcends time. And help them recognize it when they see it. Amen."

As Henry finished his blessing, Marci didn't dare look at Christopher. But she could feel him watching her—and knew he was wondering why she wasn't open to exploring the relationship everyone else in their acquaintance was pushing them toward.

To her relief, he didn't bring up the subject during the dinner. Neither did Henry. The conversation was lighthearted, and Henry's stories about his early years on Nantucket kept them laughing. It was a perfect homecoming dinner.

By the time they finished dessert, however, it was clear he was tiring. A cue Christopher picked up as well.

Setting his coffee cup back in its saucer, he smiled at Henry. "I don't know about you, but I'm ready to call it a night."

The older man checked his watch. "At seven o'clock?"

"It's been a long day."

"For me, maybe. I suspect you have some life in

you yet. Why don't you walk me in and then come back and spend a little time in my new gazebo with this pretty lady?" He winked at Marci.

Ignoring the implication, she rose, keeping her gaze fixed on the table. "If you want to get Henry settled, I'll start the cleanup."

Christopher scooted his chair back and stood. "Okay. But I'll be out in a few minutes to follow through on Henry's suggestion."

"That's my boy." Grinning at Christopher, Henry leaned on his arm as he got to his feet. Then he reached out and squeezed Marci's hand again. "Thank you again. For everything."

Warmth filled her heart as she smiled at him. "It was my pleasure, Henry."

She watched as the two men slowly crossed the yard, one tall and strong in body, the other a bit stooped and strong only in spirit. Yet they were both men of integrity and deep moral fiber, whose hearts beat with the same kindness and caring and decency. And they both considered her special.

But they were wrong, she reflected, her smile fading. She was flawed. And tainted. And sinful. She'd made bad mistakes, and though the passage of years had diminished their power to keep her awake at night, it hadn't reduced their magnitude. Nor, much to her regret, had time helped her find a way to rectify them.

Loading the tray with dishes, she hefted it up.

And thought about all the years she'd spent at Ronnie's doing this very thing as she pursued her degree and clung to the dream of a better life.

The degree had come. And when she got home, she'd find a job far away from Ronnie's. In that regard, her dream had come true.

As for any dream she might harbor about a certain doctor—it seemed far less likely to be realized.

Because based on Christopher's parting comment, he didn't intend to let the evening end without bringing up the discussion they'd tabled the night of his birthday. Meaning she was going to have to tell him about her past.

And it wasn't going to be pretty.

"Stop fussing, Christopher. I'm fine. Trust me, I'll sleep far better in my own bed than I ever did at that rest home with all those old folks. You go back out there and keep Marci company."

Smiling, Christopher picked up the medical alert button on the nightstand. "Remember this is here, Henry. And promise me you'll keep it with you whenever you're at home. That's part of the deal, okay?"

"Thanks to Patricia," he grumbled.

"I happen to agree with your daughter on this point. It's a good safety measure. If you'd had one with you when you fell, you could have called for help immediately."

"Okay, okay. I guess it's a small price to pay for independence."

"Keep that in mind." He walked to the bedroom door, stopping on the threshold to smile at the older man. "Good night. And welcome home."

"Thanks, Christopher. Now you go out there and smooth talk Marci into taking the job with Caring Connections."

"I'll do my best."

Closing the door behind him, Christopher heard the clatter of silverware against china in the kitchen. He'd honored Marci's wishes to defer the discussion about them until Henry was home, but he wasn't going to wait any longer to talk this through. He couldn't. With her departure a mere nine days away, time was running out.

"Need a hand?" He strolled into the kitchen and snagged a dish towel.

Shooting him a quick look over her shoulder, she dug back into the suds in the sink. "There isn't much left to do. We prepared everything at The Devon Rose, and I already cleaned the carrying containers and put them in my car. I'm just about finished with the china and glassware."

He picked up a plate with a delicate gold rim and an off-white embossed filigree pattern around the edge. "Did you see how Henry's eyes lit up when he realized you'd used Marjorie's good dishes?"

A soft smile touched her lips. "Yes."

"You made his homecoming special."

Shrugging, she rinsed a crystal glass. "I'm just glad he *could* come home." Turning off the water, she wiped her hands on a towel and picked up the plates Christopher had dried. "I'll put these away in the dining room."

She made several trips back and forth, and by the time she returned from her last one, Christopher was laying aside his dish towel.

"Chester said he'd come over Friday and pick up the table and chairs." Marci wiped down the counter and hung the dish rag over the faucet. "I thought Henry might want to put one of the wicker rockers from the back porch in the gazebo, with the little side table."

"I'll take care of it this weekend."

"Thanks."

She reached for her purse, and he frowned. "You aren't planning to leave, are you?"

"The party's over."

"Not according to Henry."

She gave a soft, melancholy laugh and shook her head. "He never gives up, does he?"

"No. That's one of the reasons he came home." Christopher propped a shoulder against the wall and folded his arms. "It's also one of the things he and I have in common."

She took a deep breath. The resignation—and deep sadness—in her eyes shook him.

Uncrossing his arms, he took a step toward her. "What's wrong?"

"I was hoping you'd realize our different backgrounds were a problem and let this go. That would have been easier." She closed her eyes and rubbed her forehead. "There are other reasons why this won't work, Christopher."

The cold, deadly finality of her tone left a hollow feeling in the pit of his stomach.

"Why don't we go out to the gazebo and talk about them?"

She acquiesced with a nod, but the spark that was so much a part of her seemed to have been snuffed out.

He followed her across the yard in silence. She chose the same place she'd occupied the day he'd asked her to take the job, sitting on the edge of the raised platform of the structure and setting her purse beside her.

He hadn't liked the outcome that day.

And he had a strong suspicion he wasn't going to like the outcome tonight, either.

Settling down beside her, he rested his forearms on his knees. And waited.

She didn't talk for a couple of minutes. Instead, she looked at the sea, its surface placid in the early evening. But the ocean around Nantucket was deceptive, Christopher knew. Beneath the calm veneer, rip tides and strong currents seethed, roiling the waters.

He sensed a similar inner turmoil in Marci, though her expression was composed.

"I told you about my upbringing, Christopher." Her words were soft but matter-of-fact. As if she'd distanced herself from the story she was about to tell. "My family was dirt poor and dysfunctional. After my father left and my mom died, we were even poorer. If it hadn't been for J.C., I don't know where Nathan and I would have ended up."

She inspected the blooming hydrangea beside her. Plucked a single sky-blue petal. Cradled it in her hand.

"What happened wasn't J.C.'s fault, though. He tried his best to keep Nathan and me on the straight and narrow. He could never reach Nathan, but he had better luck with me—for a while. I believed what J.C. told me—that if I worked hard I could have a better life. So I did. And it paid off. I got a scholarship to college. The day that letter came was one of the proudest of my life."

She stopped, and Christopher bit back the question that sprang to his lips. He had to give her the time and space she needed to get through her confession. And there was no doubt in his mind that's what this was.

Marci traced the edge of the fragile petal and continued. "Freshman year was great. I made excellent grades, and for the first time in my life I began to believe I had more to offer than a great body. Then I met Preston Harris III."

She lifted her hand. A few seconds later the wind plucked the petal from her palm and flung it to the ground. Wrapping her arms around herself, she studied it for a moment before transferring her gaze once more to the sea.

"Pres was the big man on campus. Good-looking, football jock, wealthy family. He noticed me for the same reason men always notice me. But he seemed different than the rest. His gifts and invitations didn't come with strings or expectations. He was the kind of man I'd always dreamed of finding. A true gentleman. I fell in love."

Tears welled in her eyes, and Christopher's heart contracted. When they spilled over, he lifted a hand to brush them away. But the instant his fingers connected with her cheek, she jerked away.

"Don't." Her voice was raw as she swiped at the tears herself. "I won't get through this if you touch me."

"Okay." He backed off, sensing she was holding on to her self-control by a thin, precarious thread.

She took a shuddering breath. "After a while, he said he loved me, too. That we'd get married when we finished school. But in the meantime, he wanted to take our relationship to the next level." She looked down at the discarded petal, which was already beginning to shrivel. "I knew it was wrong. J.C. had drummed that into me from the day I turned thirteen. But then Pres began to suggest I was using him. Taking all his gifts and dinners without ever intending to follow through. In hindsight, I realized he was manipulating me. At the time, though, I thought it was important to prove to him my love was true. So I…I gave in."

Cold anger coursed through Christopher. He'd never considered himself a violent man. But if Preston Harris III was standing here right now, he'd punch him. In a heartbeat.

"I'm sorry you had to go through that, Marci. But you're not the first woman to be taken in by a smooth talker. It doesn't change how I feel about you."

Looking back to the sea, she continued in a flat tone. "I'll spare you all the gory details. But a month later, I overheard Pres talking to one of his buddies about me. And discovered he'd never had any intention of marrying me. I was just a 'cute chick to have some fun with,' as he told his friend."

Marci blinked several times. When she resumed speaking, her voice was less steady. "I was devastated. And angry—at him and myself. I broke things off immediately and resolved never again to let anyone use me. I was also determined to move on, to consider the mistake tuition in the school of experience.

"And then I found out I was pregnant."

In the quiet that followed her whispered words, the pounding of the surf echoed the pounding of Christopher's heart. Marci's story had taken a twist he'd never expected. But shocked as he was by the news of her pregnancy, he sensed the worse was yet to come.

"When I told Pres, he suggested the baby wasn't his. That he'd always been 'careful.' And he went on to say that someone like me must have 'gotten around,' as he put it, so the father could be anyone." Her voice broke, and she sucked in a lungful of air. "But I hadn't. In fact, he was the first guy I ever… got close to."

With an abrupt move, Marci rose, crushing the discarded blue petal beneath her foot as she put some distance between them. She refolded her arms across her chest and angled slightly away from him, her fingers clenched tight on her arms.

"I didn't know what to do. I couldn't tell J.C. I didn't want him to be disappointed in me. So I talked to Nathan. He gave me some money that was probably stolen and advised me to get rid of the baby."

She was trembling now. Christopher could see that even from several feet away.

"I didn't want to do it. But I couldn't see any other option. The responsibility of a baby freaked me out. I had no way to support a child. So I had an abortion, thinking that would solve my problems. Instead, that's when they really started."

She bit her lip, and another tear began to trail

down her cheek. "I thought I could handle things afterward. But I was wrong. It tore me up inside. I dropped out of school. Drifted from city to city, working odd jobs to eke out a living, sampling the drug scene, looking for escape, running from what I'd done. That was how I lived for five years—until finally I couldn't run anymore. Couldn't deal with the emptiness of that lifestyle. In the end, I came home. Got a job at Ronnie's Diner. Went back to school. In the eyes of the world, I had my act together at last."

She bowed her head. When she continued, Christopher had to strain to hear her muted words. "But you know what? The regrets never went away. To this day, I still have dreams about the baby who never had a chance to live—because of me."

Christopher felt like someone had punched him in the jaw. He could understand how Marci had been misled by a smooth-talking campus hot shot. It happened. But as a doctor, he spent his life trying to save lives—including the most innocent of all life. That's why he'd become involved with Birthright. It was a cause in which he passionately believed.

Now he understood why Marci had looked resigned and sad earlier. She'd known her revelation could be a deal breaker.

If he wanted this relationship to have a chance, he knew what he had to do: get up, close the distance between them and pull her into his arms. Tell her that her past didn't matter to their future.

But it did.

For how could he reconcile her actions with everything he believed?

Seconds ticked by as he grappled with that dilemma.

Too many.

Marci turned toward him, the abject misery and despair in her eyes ripping at his gut.

He rose slowly. Searched for words. Came up empty.

"I need to go." Without giving him a chance to respond, Marci picked up her purse and half ran across the yard.

He started to follow. Stopped.

Less than a minute later, he heard her car engine come to life. Listened as it receded into the distance.

Christopher grasped the upright of the gazebo to steady himself as quiet descended in Henry's garden, save for the muted boom of the nearby surf. Most of the time, he considered the sound soothing. But tonight it reminded him of the distant, ominous rumble of thunder. The kind signaling an approaching storm destined to turn the world black and send sensible people scurrying to find shelter and safety.

That was how he felt now. On the precipice of a storm. The only way to remain safe, to avert the darkness Marci's departure would bring, was to welcome her into his arms.

But could he live with all the baggage she brought to the relationship?

Christopher tried to process all he'd heard. Tried to think through his options logically. But as he crossed the lawn toward his own cottage, he couldn't get the left side of his brain to cooperate.

Only his heart spoke to him, loud and clear, telling him he needed Marci in his life.

Yet making a decision this big based on emotion wasn't wise. So, as he often did when facing a monumental choice, he turned to a greater power for guidance.

Lord, please, show me what to do.

Chapter Fourteen

Someone was banging on her door.

Groaning, Marci rolled onto her back and squinted at her watch. Eight-thirty a.m. Since tears had kept her awake until dawn, that meant she'd gotten all of two hours of sleep.

"Marci! Are you in there?"

It was J.C.

She groaned again. The last thing she needed was her brother interrogating her. But why put off the inevitable.

"Yeah, yeah, hold your horses," she called.

Swinging her legs to the floor, she shoved her hair out of her eyes, padded to the door and pulled it open.

After one sweeping glance, J.C.'s grin faded. "Did I wake you?"

She tried to smother a yawn. "Yeah."

"Sorry. I figured eight-thirty was safe. I seem to recall you telling me not long ago that only slugs slept this late."

"And as you reminded me, it's okay to sleep in on vacation. It's supposed to be a time to rest and relax, right?"

"Right. Except you don't look like you've done either." He planted his fists on his hips and scrutinized her. "In fact, to put it bluntly, you look awful."

She made a face. "Thanks for the ego boost. And the purpose of this visit is?"

"Ornery today, aren't we?"

She arched an eyebrow.

"Okay, fine. I get the hint. This came for you yesterday."

As he handed over an envelope, she noted the Illinois postmark. Nathan. He'd been writing to her every week in care of The Devon Rose.

"I also wanted to remind you about having dinner with Heather and me on the beach before the fireworks," J.C. added.

She stifled another groan. She'd accepted the invitation for the Fourth of July festivities two weeks ago. But she was in no mood to celebrate after last night's conversation with Christopher.

"You know, J.C., I appreciate the invite, but I think I'll pass."

He gave her a hopeful look. "Better offer?"

"No."

He propped a shoulder against the door frame, apparently in no hurry to end the conversation. "So, how is the good doctor these days?"

"Fine."

"He was at the welcome-home dinner for Henry last night, wasn't he?"

"Yes."

"I'm surprised he didn't suggest getting together for the holiday."

He wasn't going to let this go, Marci realized. So she might as well end his speculation. And Henry's. And Edith's.

"I doubt I'll be seeing him anymore, J.C."

Her brother's brow puckered. "Why not? I got the distinct impression he was very interested in you."

"It's not a good match."

"Why not?"

"We're too different. I had dinner with him and his parents a few nights ago. They're Boston high society. His father owns a law firm. They jet all over the world. Need I say more?"

His eyes narrowed. Just as they had years ago when she'd come home from school one day crying after some girls made fun of her threadbare, thrift-store coat. "Did they snub you?"

"No. Just the opposite. They went out of their way to put me at ease. But they live in a different world, J.C. I wouldn't fit in."

He studied her in silence for a moment. "You

don't think you're good enough for people like the Morgans, do you? Well you know what? That's garbage. You're every bit as good as they are. Maybe better. You overcame tremendous odds to get where you are. It's a testament to your character that you succeeded." He raked his fingers through his hair and shook his head. "Why can't I convince you of that?"

"Trust me, J.C. It wasn't meant to be."

Anger built in his eyes. "I have a good mind to go and talk to Christopher myself. Tell him what he's missing if he lets you get away."

"No! Don't even think about it! It's *my* life. And *my* decision."

Several beats of silence ticked by as he scrutinized her. "I'm picking up some strange vibes here. Why do I sense there's something you're not telling me?"

"Because you're naturally suspicious. It must go with the detective badge. I want you to promise me you'll leave this alone."

When he clamped his jaw shut, she shot him a warning look. "Promise, J.C."

Heaving an exasperated sigh, he rubbed his neck. "You are one stubborn woman, you know that? Okay. Fine. I'll stay out of it."

"Good. Now go home to Heather. Enjoy your day while I get some more sleep."

"The invitation is still open if you change your mind about joining us later."

"Thanks."

Closing the door, Marci wandered back to the bed. It had been difficult enough to drift off in the early dawn, despite her exhaustion. No way was she going to be able to go back to sleep now, in broad daylight.

After scrunching up the pillows, she propped them behind her and sat cross-legged on the bed. Even though she'd expected rejection after Christopher heard her story, it still hurt. Badly. But that was her own fault. She'd allowed herself to believe he might be able to overlook her yesterdays. To forgive her mistakes and love her for who she was *today*.

His reaction last night, however, had proven what a pipe dream that had been. She'd never be able to escape her past. It was part of who she was, and it always would be. Perhaps if she'd met an accountant or an engineer, or someone who didn't have such a strong faith, things might have worked out better. Instead, she'd fallen for a doctor, a man committed to healing the sick and saving the unborn, whose faith was the guiding force in his life.

And if that was the kind of man who attracted her, the future looked bleak. Because based on Christopher's reaction, his kind of man wouldn't want anything to do with her kind of woman.

Overwhelmed by that depressing thought, Marci

tried to take some consolation from the letter in her hand. At least she'd repaired her relationship with Nathan. If nothing else, her brothers would always be there for her. Heather, too, she reminded herself. She was grateful J.C.'s wife treated her like a sister.

Tearing open the envelope, she withdrew the single sheet of paper and scanned the note.

Hey, Sis. Hope this reaches you by Fourth of July. I'm looking forward to celebrating my own independence day in ten months and fourteen days. (Can you tell I'm counting?)

I had a letter from J.C. last week. He mentioned you were dating a doctor on the island. That was good news. Until our talks during your visits over the past year, I never realized how my bad advice twelve years ago had affected your life. I've been praying about that, seeking forgiveness for my role in your problems. And I'm beginning to find release from the guilt.

Here's the thing, Marci. I know you feel guilty, too. And I wanted to encourage you to give it to the Lord, like I did. Let Him forgive you—and then forgive yourself. Even though none of us can change the past, I've come to believe that through prayer, we can build a better tomorrow.

You know how J.C. was after me for years to seek the Lord? Well, I'm glad I finally took his advice. It's made a huge difference in my life. It could in yours, too. If this doctor is important to you, please don't blow him off without giving the Lord a chance to touch his heart—and yours.

Take care of yourself, okay? And keep in touch.

It was signed, Love, Nathan.

Setting the letter in her lap, Marci closed her eyes. It would be wonderful to find the forgiveness Nathan spoke of. To let go of the pain and anguish that still had the power to twist her stomach into knots. But she'd never considered seeking absolution from God. She'd always felt she wasn't good enough even to ask for that.

Yet Nathan had done bad things, too. And he'd established a relationship with the Lord.

Perhaps it was worth a try.

The service she'd attended with Christopher had been a good experience, Marci recalled. There, in that small church, she'd felt the presence of a power, a force, greater than herself. And she'd also felt hope.

Rising, she tucked Nathan's letter in her purse. There was a holiday service this morning at nine. Edith had mentioned it. While there was no way she could get there in time for that, she could slip into the church afterward and visit privately with the Lord.

And maybe—just maybe—He would give a prodigal daughter the guidance and comfort she desperately needed.

The welcome aroma of fresh-brewed coffee greeted Christopher as he stepped onto Henry's back porch, bleary-eyed after his sleepless night. A shower and shave would help wake him up, but first he wanted to check on his neighbor.

Before he reached the door, Henry pushed it open. "Good morning. I saw you crossing the yard." Her gave his visitor a keen perusal. "Grab a cup of coffee and we'll sit a spell in the gazebo. You look like you could use a jolt of caffeine."

"You're right." Christopher crossed the kitchen and pulled a mug from one of the hooks under the cabinet. "But I can't say the same about you. You seem very perky this morning."

"Haven't slept that well since before I fell. Nothing like being in your own bed. Hospitals and rehab places aren't very restful."

"True." Christopher filled his mug and rejoined Henry by the door. "Take hold of my arm while we cross the yard."

"I'm not an invalid."

"And I want to keep it that way. You're recovering from major surgery, Henry. No one's as steady as usual after an operation. Use some extra caution for another couple of weeks."

His neighbor took his arm. "You're one smooth talker, you know that?"

Christopher's gut clenched. "Not always."

The older man squinted at him. "I'm not liking the sound of that. You aren't going to tell me you couldn't convince Marci to stay, are you?"

They'd arrived at the gazebo, and Christopher helped Henry step up to the platform. He waited to respond until they were both seated at the café table.

"I didn't try too hard."

The older man cocked his head. "That doesn't sound like you. Why not?"

Taking a sip of his coffee, Christopher hoped the caffeine would clear some of the cobwebs from his brain. "She gave me some reasons last night why she didn't think there was much chance things between us would work out."

"Good reasons?"

"Maybe."

"Hmph." Henry sipped his own coffee. "Family differences?"

"She brought those up, but I told her they didn't matter. It was the other things she shared that gave me pause."

"Interesting." Henry weighed his mug in his

hand. "Why do you think she did that if she thought those things might turn you away?"

Christopher frowned. He hadn't really considered her motivations. "It was the honest thing to do, I suppose."

"Indeed it was. Seems to me that shows a lot of integrity. And courage." Henry took a slow sip of coffee. "When you love someone, you do things for them that aren't always in your own best interest. You try to protect them. To do what's best for *them*."

Christopher looked at his neighbor. "No one ever said anything about love."

"Not in words, maybe. But anyone who's ever loved can recognize it in someone else. And I've been seeing plenty of it right here in my own backyard." He set his mug on the table and leaned forward. "Marci didn't have to tell you her secrets, yet she chose to let you see the whole package before you got too involved. Even at the risk of losing you."

Christopher wrapped his fingers around his mug and stared into the dark liquid. Henry was right. He knew Marci's feelings ran as strong and deep as his. He could see it in her eyes.

Just as he'd seen the reflection of her breaking heart when she'd turned toward him after he'd rejected her.

And that's what his silence in the aftermath of her revelation had been, he acknowledged.

Rejection.

As loud and clear as if he'd spoken the words.

A sudden wave of nausea swept over him. He'd never wanted to hurt Marci. The Lord knew she'd been hurt too much already in her life. What he wanted to do was love her.

But how was he supposed to deal with her past?

"I don't know what she told you last night, Christopher, but I can see it's got you tied up in knots." Henry laid a hand on his shoulder. "Must have been a powerful story. You in the mood to hear another one?"

Curious, Christopher gave his full attention to the man who'd become a second grandfather to him. "Sure."

Settling back in his chair, Henry took a measured sip of his coffee and surveyed the horizon, where a distant boat churned purposefully forward, maintaining a steady course. "You know about my service in Korea."

"Some. You've never given me much detail."

"That's because most of it was ugly. I told you once a lot of the guys I served with were haunted by the memories for the rest of their lives. I didn't tell you why. But I think it's time you knew."

Henry set his mug on the table and folded his hands over his stomach. "Korea was a bad place, Christopher. Most of the American foot soldiers were young, undertrained, underequipped and unprepared. We were dealing with an aggressive enemy, plus a huge refugee population that the North Korean soldiers often mingled with—in disguise. After they got behind American lines, they'd conduct guerrilla operations. As you might imagine, it was a very tense situation, and we were always watching our backs."

His lips settled into a grim line, and he fell silent as he gazed again toward the sea. In all the months he'd known the older man, Christopher had never seen such distress tighten his features. It was almost as if he was in physical pain.

"You don't have to tell me this, Henry."

His neighbor looked back at him. "Yes, I do. For Marci's sake."

Twin furrows creased Christopher's brow. "What do your experiences in Korea have to do with Marci?"

"You'll see in a few minutes. I hope." Henry took a deep breath. "We'd been told to consider refugees hostile and to keep them off the roads. We'd also been told to search them whenever they crossed our path.

"One day we saw a dozen or more approaching. We called to them to halt. They didn't. We tried again. Same result. There were only a few of us on that patrol, and we were nervous. The day before some of our buddies had been killed or wounded by enemy soldiers who'd infiltrated a group just like the one we were facing."

He swallowed. Picked up his coffee. His hand was trembling as he took a sip and set it carefully back on the table.

"As they drew closer, one of them reached inside their coat. I panicked and pulled the trigger. Chaos erupted. More shots were fired. The refugees scattered, what was left of them. Eight were killed by me and my fellow soldiers. After things finally quieted down, we checked them out. Five were women. Two were old men. One was a child. The person I shot was a woman. I thought she'd been reaching inside her coat for a weapon. But when I opened it, I found a baby. Also dead."

In the silence following Henry's story, Christopher tried to imagine the stomach-churning horror of that moment.

It was beyond his comprehension.

Nor could he reconcile the frail, tender-hearted older man beside him with the terrified young soldier who'd pulled the trigger that spawned a massacre.

But the deep, gut-wrenching sadness in Henry's eyes confirmed they were one and the same.

"I never told that story to anyone except Marjorie, Christopher. And I almost didn't tell it to her. I was ashamed, and I thought she'd reject me if she knew what I'd done. But in the end, I couldn't in good conscience ask her to marry me without letting her see into my soul, with all its dark places. I had to take that risk. It was the only fair thing to do."

At last Christopher found his voice. "What did she say?"

The whisper of a smile tugged at Henry's lips. "I'll never forget it. She took my hand, looked me in the eye and said, 'You were young, Henry. And afraid. You were trying to protect yourself in a hostile environment. Yes, you made a tragic mistake. But when I look into your heart I see only kindness and caring and empathy. I know you would never hurt anyone out of malice or anger. Your spirit is too gentle. That's why I love you. And that will never change. So make your peace with the Lord. And then let it go. As I intend to.'"

As Henry's words echoed in the quiet air, Christopher thought about Marjorie's eloquent declaration of love. She'd looked into Henry's heart and known that only extraordinary circumstances would have caused him to act in such an uncharacteristic manner.

He hadn't cut Marci the same slack.

But he should have. She, too, had been young and afraid, ill-equipped and unprepared for the challenge she'd faced. Like Henry, she'd panicked and pulled the trigger—in a figurative sense—cutting short a life. And she'd lived with guilt and regret ever since.

Settling his elbows on the table, he dropped his head into his hands.

"I really blew it, didn't I?"

"It's not too late to make things right."

He shook his head, feeling as bleak as a gray winter day on Nantucket. "It might be."

"Nope. Marci will give you another chance. That's the kind of woman she is. Some people go through fire and get burned so badly their scars never heal. Others are forged by fire in a good way. I don't know what Marci told you. What bad experiences she had or bad decisions she made. But I do know she has a kind and forgiving heart."

He smiled and leaned close to once more rest his hand on Christopher's shoulder. "I know one other thing, too. Whether she's ready to admit it or not, she loves you. And love changes everything."

For a long moment, Christopher regarded the older man. Then, picking up his mug, he stood. "I think I need to take a little drive into town. Would you like me to help you inside before I leave?"

"No. I'm going to stay here and do some reminiscing. But I want a full report later."

"Wish me luck."

"I'll do that." Henry lifted his mug in salute. "But you do your part, too. Letting that little lady get away would be foolish. And you're no fool, my friend."

Maybe not, Christopher thought as he strode across the lawn toward his cottage. But he'd sure acted like one with Marci. He could only pray she would be as generous and forgiving as Henry expected.

Even if he didn't deserve it.

"Well, look who's here!"

At the sound of Edith's voice, Marci glanced toward the door of the church as her landlords crossed the lawn, aiming for the bench where she sat.

"Hi, Edith. Chester."

The older man gave her a shy smile and dipped his head.

"What brings you to church today?" Edith asked.

"Just paying a visit. But I was too late for the service, so I thought I'd wait out here until it was over."

"You could have come in. God doesn't give out tardy slips." The older woman chuckled. "But you go right on in now. The place will be cleared out in a matter of minutes. Everyone has holiday plans. See you later."

Commandeering Chester's arm, she towed him along toward their car.

Marci waited five more minutes, then slipped inside the empty church, choosing a pew near the back.

For a long while she simply sat there, letting the peaceful ambiance soothe her. She'd experienced this same sense of reassurance on her last visit, too. And it felt good.

After fifteen or twenty minutes, she pulled a piece of printed material from the rack on the pew in front of her and began paging through it. It was a guide for today's service, she realized.

All at once, a quote from Ephesians jumped off the page at her.

"I pray that the eyes of your heart may be enlightened, so that you will know what is the hope of His calling."

How odd. It was as if J.C. or Nathan were talking to her. Both of her brothers were always praying she'd see the light.

The imagery of the passage was nice, too, Marci reflected, reading it a second time. *The eyes of your heart.* How apt. For the heart did see. Often more clearly than the eye. She also liked the reference to finding hope in the call of the Lord. That had happened with Nathan last year. Once he'd heard the Lord's call, his life had been transformed.

Maybe it was her turn now. Better late than never, right? After all, Edith had just told her the Lord didn't give out tardy slips.

Marci took a deep breath. What could it hurt to try? Worst case, He would reject her. And she was used to that.

Feeling a little awkward, she bowed her head and closed her eyes.

Okay, Lord, here I am. In Your house. You don't know me very well, but my brothers are friends of Yours. You've probably heard them mention my name a few hundred times. Sorry about that. They can be annoyingly persistent.

Anyway, here's the thing. There's this guy I like. Christopher Morgan. I talked to You once before about him. He likes me. Or he did. Until I told him about all the mistakes I've made.

I'm sorry about those, Lord. Sorrier than I can say. If I had a chance to relive all those bad years, I'd make different decisions. But I can't. All I can do is lay them in front of You and ask Your forgiveness. J.C. is always telling me how kind and merciful You are. How You're willing to give people a second chance, and how You value people for what's inside their hearts, not for the clothes they wear or the money they have. I wish more humans were like You.

So if You're really like that, You know my remorse is sincere. And You know I've tried very hard in the past seven years to live a good life. To be a good person. Maybe You can help me be even better. I'm willing to work with you on this, Lord. I want to be good enough to be loved by someone who's kind and caring and decent and generous. Someone like Christopher.

If you could show me how to...

"Marci?"

So focused was she on her thoughts that it took a couple of seconds for the resonant baritone voice beside her to register. When it did, her eyes flew open.

Christopher stood in the aisle, dressed in khaki slacks and an open-necked blue shirt that matched his eyes. But he wasn't his usual put-together self. He'd missed one of his buttons, his hair was damp and a bit tousled from a very recent shower and he'd nicked his chin shaving.

Nevertheless, he looked fabulous to her.

"May I join you?" He motioned toward the pew.

She slid over, noting the smudges beneath his lower lashes and the lines of strain around his mouth. Apparently he hadn't slept any better than she had.

"What are you doing here?" She clenched her hands in her lap and gave him a wary look.

"Looking for you. I stopped by the cottage, and Edith told me where you were. Good thing I ran into her. I would never have thought to check here."

A mirthless smile twisted her lips. "Yeah. Marci Clay in a church. Imagine that. I'm surprised God hasn't tossed me out on my ear."

He frowned. "That's not what I meant."

"Maybe not. But it's true."

"God welcomes everyone, Marci. Even people who make mistakes. Like me."

She shot him a skeptical glance. "You haven't made any mistakes that I've noticed."

"I made a big one last night when I let you walk away."

Her heart did a little quickstep, but she ruthlessly smothered the tiny ember of hope that ignited. She'd indulged in romantic fantasies about Christopher once; she wouldn't set herself up like that again.

"You did the right thing. You deserve better than me."

"Marci." He angled toward her, and when he took her hands the touch of his strong, lean fingers set her pulse racing. "Give yourself more credit than that. You're a very special woman. You're smart and caring and funny and strong and kind. You have a generous, loving heart. And you've added an incredible spark to my life." His eyes grew soft, and she could read the apology in their depths. "I should have said all that last night, and I'm sorry I didn't. My only excuse is that you walked away before I could process everything you told me."

She tried to think, but the warmth of his fingers was short-circuiting her brain. "I did dump a lot on you."

"Maybe. But I've had all night to think about it. And here's where I stand. I know our relationship is new, and I'm not suggesting we rush this. What

I'd like you to do is stay and take the director job with Caring Connections. Give me a chance to court you properly. Then let's put the rest in God's hands and see where He leads us. What do you say?"

As Marci gazed into his warm blue eyes, her lungs stopped working. Was it possible that all she'd hoped and prayed for had been granted? It seemed too good to be true.

"Why, Christopher?" She searched his eyes. "Why do you want me, after all the mistakes I made?"

"No one is exempt from making mistakes, Marci. And making them doesn't mean we're bad people. It just means we used bad judgment. All we can do is learn from them, move on and try to do better. That's what God asks of us. And that's what you did. How can I expect anything more?" He stroked his thumb along the back of her hand, creating a trail of warmth. "As Henry reminded me this morning, I'd be a fool to let you go. I agree. So please…say you'll stay."

At his husky request, Marci felt the pressure of tears in her throat. Listening to her heart at last, she took the leap. "Okay." The word came out in a croak.

Relief smoothed the tension from Christopher's face, and he stood, tugging her to her feet. "Come with me."

"Where are we going?" She followed as he led

her down the aisle and out the front door, into the dazzling sun of a glorious Nantucket morning.

Guiding her to the side of the porch, behind the privacy of a tall hydrangea bush laden with blossoms, he pulled her into his arms. "To seal our bargain."

Before she could respond, he gave her a kiss that communicated more eloquently than words the joy and love that was in his heart.

When at last he released her, settling his hands at her waist while she clung to his neck, he grinned. "What are your plans for the rest of the day?"

"I don't have any."

"You do now. Ending with fireworks."

Marci smiled and traced his lips with a whisper stroke of her finger. "I just had my fireworks."

At her touch, his eyes darkened. "How about an encore?"

Bending down once more, his mouth settled over hers in a kiss that spoke of promises and hope and a new tomorrow. Never had Marci felt so cherished.

For Christopher's love hadn't simply filled her world with joy. It had also liberated her from the shadows of her past.

It was a gift she would treasure every day of her life.

Just as she would treasure the special man who'd given her an Independence Day to remember.

Epilogue

❧

Five Months Later

As Marci drove toward 'Sconset in the deepening dusk, a contented smile curved her lips. It was hard to believe how fairy-tale-like her life had become in the past few months. She felt like Cinderella. Except the ball hadn't ended at midnight.

Caring Connections was up and running, and public reception and support had been phenomenal.

Her job as director gave her everything she'd ever hoped to find in a career—satisfaction, joy and the contentment of knowing she was doing meaningful work that made a difference in people's lives.

J.C. and Heather were close by, and in five months Nathan would join them to complete their original little circle.

She'd made new friends like Edith and Chester and Henry—whom she was visiting today.

Her journey to the Lord was progressing well, imbuing her days with a new sense of purpose and hope.

And then there was Christopher.

As large, lazy flakes of snow began to fall, adding a pristine topping to the already white world, her smile broadened.

Month by month, their relationship had deepened and flourished. If ever she'd harbored doubts about their ability to reconcile their different backgrounds, they'd vanished. Christopher had made it clear in every word and every action that he valued her for who she was. All her old baggage had been relegated to the basement—where it belonged.

After making the turn onto Henry's lane, Marci eased the car to a stop in front of his cottage. Warm light shone from the windows, and a cranberry wreath hung on the door. Through the front window she could see the tree she and Christopher had helped him decorate last weekend in anticipation of the holiday. Although Patricia had invited him to spend Christmas in Boston, he'd chosen to stay in his snug cottage and celebrate the day at The Devon Rose with Marci's family, joined by Christopher and Edith and Chester.

Stepping out of the car, Marci rounded the hood,

the snow crunching under her boots. It wasn't windy, but the air was cold and she was glad she'd wrapped a scarf around her neck and worn gloves and earmuffs.

As she approached the front door, she spied a note taped to the front.

"Knob's being cranky. Come around back."

Odd. The knob had seemed okay two days ago.

Switching direction, Marci headed for the gate that led to the backyard. Good thing there was a retired carpenter in 'Sconset on her Caring Connections resource list. She made a mental note to send him over tomorrow to check it out.

As she covered the short distance to the arbor, she noted that someone had shoveled a narrow path. Hopefully not Henry. He'd been doing great; the last thing he needed was another fall.

Pushing through the gate, she blinked a snowflake off her eyelash and lifted her face to the heavens. A few stars were beginning to twinkle in the distance where the sky was clearing, while above her lazy flakes continued to sift down from the indigo expanse.

It was lovely. And peaceful. Only the muted sound of the surf broke the stillness.

That is, until the hushed strains of "I'll Be Home For Christmas" suddenly drifted through the quiet air from the back of Henry's cottage.

Curious, she continued toward the rear. But as she rounded the corner, she came to an abrupt halt.

For the scene before her was pure magic.

Outlined with glowing white twinkle lights and bedecked with boughs of greenery and large red bows, Henry's gazebo had been transformed into an enchanting winter wonderland.

And waiting for her inside was the man of her dreams. Dressed in jeans and a fleece-lined suede coat, he gave her a smile that warmed her to her core despite the frosty air.

Moving forward, she stopped at the edge of the structure. "Hi."

"Hi." The appealing, husky tenor of his voice sent her pulse tripping into double time.

"Did you do this?" She gestured around the gazebo.

"I did the work. Henry supervised."

"Why?"

He extended his hand, and when she took it, he tugged her up beside him. "Because this gazebo represents love. And I couldn't think of a more appropriate place to propose."

She stared at him. For weeks she'd known they were headed in this direction. But she hadn't expected it to happen this soon.

Before she could gather her thoughts, Christopher cradled both her hands in his. "I know we said we'd take things slowly. But we've known each other seven months now. And I've never been more sure about anything. I want to spend the rest of my life with you, Marci. If you prefer to wait a while to get married, I can live with that—as long as I have a date to look forward to."

Backing up a step, he urged her into a chair that looked a lot like the ones around Henry's kitchen table. Then he dropped to one knee in front of her and took her hand in his. The love shining in his eyes tightened her throat, and she blinked to clear the mist from her vision.

"Marci Clay, I love you with all my heart, and I promise you I always will. For better or worse, in good times and bad. Just like these Christmas lights have illuminated Henry's gazebo, you add light to my life every day of the year. Will you do me the honor of becoming my wife?"

Joy overflowed in Marci's heart, and with a hand that wasn't quite steady, she touched his face in wonder. If she lived to be a hundred, she would never forget this moment, when he'd offered her the greatest blessing she could ever hope to receive— the gift of his love forever.

"Yes." Her response came out in a whispered cloud of frosty breath.

He smiled, closed his eyes, and let out a long, relieved sigh. "Thank You, Lord."

"You didn't think I'd say no, did you?"

"A man never knows for sure until he hears the

word." Standing, he pulled her to her feet, his expression jubilant. "What do you say we warm up our lips?"

She gave him an impish grin. "Were you thinking about having some hot chocolate?"

"Maybe later. I had a faster method in mind." Pulling her into the circle of his arms, he shot a quick glance over her shoulder toward Henry's cottage and smiled down at her. "I have to warn you. We probably have an audience."

"I don't mind if you don't. Henry had a lot to do with bringing about this happy ending."

"True. Plus, he has a vested interest in the outcome."

"How so?"

"He and I had a long talk while we decorated the gazebo. He said his cottage is getting too big for him, and he offered to sell it to me—or, I should say, to us—and move next door to the guest cottage. With one caveat. We have to give him unlimited access to the garden and gazebo. What do you think?"

She smiled. "I think it's perfect."

"Then how about we set his mind at ease?"

She wrapped her arms around his neck and tugged him close, until their faces were only a whisper apart. "Let's."

Bending down, he sealed their engagement in the most traditional of ways as the melodic words of the carol drifted through the night air.

I'll be home for Christmas, if only in my dreams.

And as she lost herself in the magic of his kiss, Marci gave thanks. For here, in Christopher's arms, her dreams had come true.

She was home.

For always.

* * * * *

Dear Reader,

I'm so glad you joined me for another stroll down Lighthouse Lane!

When I conceived this series, I didn't know that any of the books would feature siblings. But then I met the Clay family. And after J.C. introduced me to his sister and brother, I knew I had to write their stories, too. So my Lighthouse Lane series grew from three books to four.

I loved writing Marci and Christopher's story. And I loved how they discovered—with a little help from Henry!—that despite their blue-collar vs. blue-blood backgrounds, they were meant for each other. Wouldn't it be great if we all had a wise and wonderful grandfather figure like Henry in our lives?

To learn more about my books, I invite you to visit my Web site at www.irenehannon.com. And please watch for Nathan's story, the final installment in my Lighthouse Lane series, coming in April 2010. It's called *A Father for Zach*.

In the meantime, I wish all of you a wonderful new year. May it glow with the magic of white twinkle lights—just like Henry's gazebo!

Irene Hannon

QUESTIONS FOR DISCUSSION

1. In this novel, Marci suffers from low self-esteem. Have you ever struggled with self-esteem? How did that affect your life? What does Scripture say about the value of each person?

2. Christopher doesn't offer assistance to Marci when he sees her crying in the restaurant because he was burned once before when he was being a good Samaritan. Have you ever had a bad experience that kept you from following the dictates of your faith? Describe the situation. Does it still have an impact on your actions?

3. Our society holds physical attractiveness as a high ideal. Yet it backfired with Marci. Talk about the downside of being beautiful. Have you ever dated anyone who was attracted to you for the wrong reasons? How did you deal with it?

4. Marci has a close relationship with her brothers. Why do you think her family connections are important to her? Do you have a close relationship with your siblings? Why or why not?

5. Christopher has forged a strong relationship with Henry. Why do the two men get along so well? Describe some of the things they've done to solidify their friendship.

6. Why do you think Marci volunteered to help Henry put his garden in order? What does this say about her?

7. When sparks begin to fly between Marci and Christopher, neither wants to pursue the attraction. Talk about the reasons why each thinks a relationship is a bad idea. Are any of those reasons valid? Why or why not?

8. When Henry is injured, Christopher tells Marci about his own grandfather's experience in an assisted-living facility and that he wants to help Henry remain independent. Do you think his strong feelings are justified? Why or why not? Have you ever had any experience with an assisted-living facility?

9. Henry's daughter Patricia suspects Marci of ulterior motives for helping her father. What does this say about Henry's daughter?

10. When Henry begins to lose hope, Marci comes up with an idea to give him something joyous

to anticipate. Why is it important in life to have something to look forward to? What does the Bible tell us about facing the future?

11. Denise threatened suicide if Christopher ended their relationship. Marci called that emotional blackmail. Have you ever experienced manipulative behavior? How did you deal with it?

12. Why do you think Marci avoided reaching out to God for so long, despite her brother's urging to give faith a try? In light of her life experiences, what might you have said to try and persuade her to establish a relationship with the Lord?

13. In his office, and again at dinner with his parents, Marci hears about Christopher's involvement with Birthright…and she doesn't think he'll ever be able to forgive what she's done. Nor can she forgive herself. Have you ever known anyone who's had an abortion? How did it affect her life?

14. When Marci prays in church at the end of the book, she says that if she had it to do over again, she'd make different decisions. Have you ever made an important decision that you later regretted? How did you come to terms with it? How did it affect your life?

15. At the end of the book, Christopher's love liberates Marci from the shadows of her past. Do you see love as liberating or confining? As a burden or a blessing? Can it be both? Talk about the qualities that constitute a healthy, sustaining love.

Scandal surrounds Rebecca Gunderson after she shares a storm cellar during a deadly tornado with Pete Benjamin. No one believes the time she spent with him was totally innocent. Can Pete protect her reputation?

Read on for a sneak peek of
HEARTLAND WEDDING by Renee Ryan,
Book 2 in the AFTER THE STORM:
THE FOUNDING YEARS *series*
available February 2010
from Love Inspired Historical.

"Marry me," Pete demanded, realizing his mistake as the words left his mouth. He hadn't asked her. He'd told her.

He tried to rectify his insensitive act but Rebecca was already speaking over him. "Why are you willing to spend the rest of your life married to a woman you hardly know?"

"Because it's the right thing to do," he said.

Angling her head, she caught her bottom lip between her teeth and then did something utterly remarkable. She smoothed her fingertips across his forehead. "As sweet as I think your gesture is, you don't have to save me."

A pleasant warmth settled over him at her touch, leaving him oddly disoriented. "Yes, I do."

She dropped her hand to her side. "I don't mind what others say about me. You and I, *we*, know the truth."

Pete caught her hand in his, and turned it over in his palm. "I told Matilda Johnson we were getting married."

She snatched her hand free. "You…you…*what?*"

He spoke more slowly this time. "I told her we were getting married."

She did *not* like his answer. That much was made clear by her scowl. "You shouldn't have done that."

"She was blaming you for luring me into my own storm cellar."

The color leached out of Rebecca's cheeks as she sank into a nearby chair. "I…I simply don't know what to say."

"Say yes. Mrs. Johnson is a bully. Our marriage will silence her. I'll speak with the pastor today and—"

"No."

"—schedule the ceremony at once." His words came to a halt. "What did you say?"

"I said, no." She rose cautiously, her palms flat on her thighs as though to brace herself. "I won't marry you."

"You're turning me down? After everything that's happened today?"

"No. I mean, *yes*. I'm turning you down."

"Your reputation—"

"Is my concern, not yours."

She sniffed, rather loudly, but she didn't give in to her emotions. Oh, she blinked. And blinked. And *blinked*. But no tears spilled from her eyes.

Pete pulled in a hard breath. He'd never been more baffled by a woman. "We were both in my storm cellar," he reminded her through a painfully tight jaw. "That means we share the burden of the consequences equally."

Blink, blink, blink. "My decision is final."

"So is mine. We'll be married by the end of the day."

Her breathing quickened to short, hard pants. And then…*at last*…it happened. One lone tear slipped from her eye.

"Rebecca, please," he whispered, knowing his soft manner came too late.

"No." She wrapped her dignity around her like a coat of iron-clad armor. "We have nothing more to say to each other."

Just as another tear plopped onto the toe of her shoe, she turned and rushed out of the kitchen.

Stunned, Pete stared at the empty space she'd occupied. "That," he said to himself, "could have gone better."

* * * * *

Will Pete be able to change Rebecca's mind
and salvage her reputation?
Find out in HEARTLAND WEDDING
available in February 2010
only from Love Inspired Historical.

Copyright © 2010 by Renee M. Halverson

Love Inspired®
SUSPENSE
RIVETING INSPIRATIONAL ROMANCE

Watch for our new series of
edge-of-your-seat suspense novels.
These contemporary tales
of intrigue and romance
feature Christian characters
facing challenges to their faith...
and their lives!

NOW AVAILABLE IN REGULAR
& LARGER-PRINT FORMATS

Steeple
Hill®

Visit:
www.SteepleHill.com

LISUSDIR10

Love Inspired
HISTORICAL

INSPIRATIONAL HISTORICAL ROMANCE

Engaging stories of romance,
adventure and faith,
these novels are set in
various historical periods
from biblical times
to World War II.

NOW AVAILABLE!

**Steeple
Hill®**

For exciting stories that reflect traditional values,
visit:
www.SteepleHill.com

LIHDIR08